George Le Grand

Western India

outlook

George Le Grand

Western India

Reprint of the original, first published in 1871.

1st Edition 2022 | ISBN: 978-3-36812-661-2

Verlag (Publisher): Outlook Verlag GmbH, Zeilweg 44, 60439 Frankfurt, Deutschland
Vertretungsberechtigt (Authorized to represent): E. Roepke, Zeilweg 44, 60439 Frankfurt, Deutschland
Druck (Print): Books on Demand GmbH, In de Tarpen 42, 22848 Norderstedt, Deutschland

WESTERN INDIA

BEFORE AND DURING THE MUTINIES:

PICTURES DRAWN FROM LIFE.

BY

MAJOR-GENERAL SIR GEORGE LE GRAND JACOB

K.C.S.I., C.B.

Late Special Political Commissioner, Southern Mahratta Country,
etc.

LONDON:

HENRY S. KING & CO., 65 CORNHILL.

1871.

TO

MY NIECE AND ADOPTED DAUGHTER

GERTRUDE L. JACOB,

WITHOUT WHOSE HELP

A BLIND AND INFIRM OLD MAN COULD NOT

HAVE ATTEMPTED EVEN THIS PARTIAL

RECORD OF A TRYING PUBLIC LIFE.

CONTENTS

———◦◦◦———

Contents.

WESTERN INDIA

BEFORE AND DURING THE MUTINIES.

(PICTURES DRAWN FROM LIFE.)

———◦◊◦———

CHAPTER I.

INTRODUCTORY OBSERVATIONS.

I HAVE met with no.work giving full insight into the duties and responsibilities of Indian Political officers, a body of men who uphold British supremacy or British interests over some fifty millions of human beings, and whether as Residents at native Courts, or under the titles of Commissioner, Agent, or Superintendent, with their respective Deputies and Assistants, control, with more or less of diplomacy or of direct power, both

B

kings and people.　In the larger States, under treaty
engagements, their duties are mainly diplomatic ;
but even in these, large classes have come in some
measure under British protection by guarantees
and stipulations, so that the Ambassador becomes
a perpetual umpire in disputes between the Crown
and its subjects, to an extent calling for great
discrimination and tact: and where the power of
the Crown has become too weak to enforce its
jurisdiction, Criminal Courts have been established,
of which the British Agent is *ex officio* Chief Judge
—in many cases the Raja retaining only his title
and honours, the Englishman performing his duties.
This brief statement shows the important part our
Indian Politicals have to play, whether in preserving peace or in aiding war.　In the first case, they
oppose British prejudices, and are exposed to the
charge of pandering to those of the natives.　In
the second, they have to witness the success their
exertions have aided or perhaps brought about,
attributed to others ; well for them, indeed, if they
are not also thought marplots by the very troops
of which they may have been the guiding spirit.

An anecdote will show the current feeling, as a straw how the wind blows.

On the gathering together of the force for our first great struggle in the Punjab, Major Broadfoot was the Political authority endeavouring to bring the 'Khalsa' to reason. He was a man of great ability, and was justly lamented in the public notice of his death issued by the Governor-General.

'Them Politicals spoils all,' said one soldier to another, as they marched along towards the battle ground; 'we shall yet have all our trouble for nothing with their palavering.' To which his comrade replied, smacking his hand on the eighteen-pounder they were escorting: 'Them's your Politicals; a fig for other sorts!' There is much of homely truth in this view of things. Force is the *ultima ratio* on which human empire is based; but it is moral as well as physical, and has to be wielded skilfully to be of use.

Owing to the large field for selection offered by the Military services of India, and the training so many undergo in the extra regimental duties on which they are employed, the Political Department has been mainly recruited from the army, though the Civil services have also furnished brilliant names, such as Metcalfe and Elphinstone.

As regards their duties in maintaining peace and order, these are, unhappily for mankind, far less appreciated than those of war. It is easy to pick a quarrel and give plausible reasons for so doing; honours are then showered down on the successful parties, whilst men who have endeavoured to save bloodshed, and have succeeded, remain unknown. *Valuable goods received and no questions asked,* may be a maxim calculated to enrich a pawnbroker, but it is ill suited to a Christian Throne desirous of maintaining moral supremacy over its distant possessions. With the tendency in high places to reward strife and overlook the labours of peace, greater is the praise due to the large class that has done so much to secure the latter throughout the great continent of India. Had Sir A. Burnes's advice been listened to, there would have been no disastrous campaign in Afghanistan, though Sir John Keane might have missed a barony: had Sir James Outram not been summarily ejected, and the reins given over to a clever soldier, no contest in Sind, though Sir Charles Napier would have been without his hundred thousand pounds and the army its rich prize-money. The first is not a case exactly in point, because happening in a foreign and independent country; the second is pre-eminently so, and might be borne out by many instances in other parts of India less known to fame. It is to the honour of the Indian Political service that, as a body, it has always advocated peace rather than war, and stood up for British good faith with allies and tributaries, as of more value than British aggrandisement. Yet no men have struck harder or more effectual blows when such became necessary and just.

State pageants and processions, durbars, nautches, fights of elephants and wild beasts, have been written of in abundance. But the daily work, the subtle intrigue, the wild superstitions to be dealt with, the indoor dress, as it were, of an Indian Political's life, are little known.

My original intention was to give in chronological order a series of historic pictures from a journal kept during the greater part of half a century. But blindness and broken health have compelled me to pass over many years in silence, that before entire prostration, I might place on record facts connected with the great rising of 1857–58, because, strange to say, they have been denied both in Parliament and by the press, and as few of the official documents of the time have seen the light, are generally unknown.

The safety of our position in India is greatly lessened by this ignorance. We have been too apt to regard increase of territory as increase of power, and to study the wishes of the governing nation rather than the feelings of the governed. As long as kingdom after kingdom was added to the Empire, our laws imposed on the people, their religions discountenanced, and our manufactures permitted to drive theirs out of their own markets, all was thought to go swimmingly on. Nobody cared to ask what the natives thought about all this. It needed such an awakening as that of the years mentioned, to teach us a wiser policy. But if the British people are kept in ignorance of the nature and extent of that crisis, the scare of what they do know will soon pass away, and the lesson have been taught in vain. Some who ought to know better, maintain that there was no rebellion at all, only a partial mutiny caused solely by the greased cartridge. Others that, besides the said mutiny, there were a few local insurrections, un-connected with it. On which plea the troops of Madras and Bombay *not reporting to the Horse Guards Commander-in-Chief,*[1] were for several years refused the medals they had won and have since received. Some have gone so far as to assert that the chiefs and people were nearly everywhere on our side. There is danger of these opinions gaining ground, chiming in as they do with our self-love and our land hunger, unless those qualified by personal knowledge speak out.

We found by bitter experience that it would not do to govern distant populations against their will; and, having learnt that lesson, allow our

---

[1] The one in Bengal is alone recognised as such at the War Office, though he has, or at any rate had, no control over the Madras and Bombay Armies.

colonies to legislate for themselves. Yet we have dealt with the millions of India without ascertaining their feelings: on the one hand, as if they were mere savages; on the other, as though the laws that suit us must necessarily suit them. This was done more especially from the expiration of the old Company's Charter in 1833 to the explosion of 1857, during which time the prevailing policy was to spread the red colour on the map over the whole continent of India.

In proof of our national onesidedness, let us take a very recent act of an able Governor-General who, desiring to ascertain the relative value to the people of British and native rule, called for the opinions of our own functionaries only. Surely, if we wish to know whether or not the shoe pinches, we should rather ask the wearer than the maker. An anecdote seems in point. Every old Indian sportsman knows the reputation enjoyed by Stunt's shoes. I owe my life to a pair during a tussle with a wild boar, and on taking my home furlough went to him, as a matter of course, for a pedestrian outfit. Having become somewhat crippled therefrom, I applied for remedial measures, and was surprised, if not amused, by being told 'it was all the fault of the *fut.*' In vain were my remarks that it was generally considered rather the business of the shoe to fit the foot than the foot the shoe; the angry foreman replied that their articles were made on scientific principles, from which he had no idea of swerving. Of course I went elsewhere for my wants, and found an equally scientific but more practical artist in Bann of Bond Street, who made a point of ascertaining where the shoe pinched and why; and thus providing for any little peculiarity, up to the time of his firm passing away, enabled me in comfort to take what exercise I pleased.

Why will not our rulers adopt the Bann rather than the Stunt policy—that is, endeavour to find out the tender points of native character, and make due allowance for them? The question is more applicable to the period above alluded to—preceding 1857—than since, but there is still great room for improvement. Had we acted persistently on this policy—one, indeed, that gained our footing in India—we might have obtained better discipline in our Sepoys, and have been spared the horrors of the great outbreak.

Our measures may be very scientific, but the question is, Do we want to preserve our *clientelle?*

We are hurrying on measures that entail heavy outlay and increased taxation, and legislating far too rapidly for a people so thoroughly engrained with conservatism as are the Hindoos. Accustomed only to patriarchal government, they would willingly rather pay a bad tax, if paid by their forefathers, than one, however theoretically superior, that was new to them.[1] I grant the difficulty of ascertaining

[1] The following extract of a recent letter from a very intelligent native friend, a well-wisher to our rule, is to the point :—

' I trust the E. I. Association may be able to watch the progress of the Committee now sitting. . . . I think the financial policy of the Government has done and is doing a great deal of mischief. Development in India means more taxes, and more departments, and nothing more. . . . Government should not betake itself to cotton growing and breeding cattle. The freest market is the cheapest, and in India no market can possibly be free wherein the Government is a grower and seller.

' So long as the taxes reached only the higher classes there was not much to fear. But now the area has been widened and the sweep goes deeper than it ever did before. The masses are too simple to understand decentralisation and federalisation, but they see the taxes plainly enough. Even some of the repealed taxes are being revived

the feelings of so multifarious a community, the greater part but half civilised, and at best holding a civilisation entirely foreign to our own. Still it is not impossible; and each year as we rear natives capable of understanding and appreciating both states, the task will become easier. But there have never been wanting Englishmen of cosmo-politan character and generous sympathies, en-abling them to gain the confidence of the people they ruled over or dwelt amongst, whose voice has been raised to warn Government of the danger it was courting. It was not their fault if they cried in vain, if their voice was classed with that of others advocating more than just deference to native usages; or lost amid the din of arms, the clamour of men supposing the cause of Christianity ad-vanced by measures that led to its being hated; above all, because of the lust of power.

under different names. We have irrigation, railways, surveys, forests, and what-not; and all go to swell the number of taxes.

'All this arises from over government and hot-house legislation. I must say that I find it hard to keep pace with what goes on. What the common people must be thinking and doing may easily be con-ceived. I am sorry to say there is no hand able and willing to stay or slacken the progress of the legislative car.

'Let me assure you that the speed is getting positively dangerous.'

I have long hoped to read a full account of the 'Sepoy War' by one so thoroughly qualified to give it as the historian Kaye, whose recent nomination, by the way, to the Star of India does quite as much honour to the order as to himself. There are men who gain nothing by a handle to their names, and his past writings stamp him as one such. But time draws on. I shall probably pass away before his history is completed, if indeed it ever be so; wherefore, while still able in some degree to record my testimony, I stand before my countrymen as a witness to facts.

CHAPTER II.

FEMALE RULERS.

IT is not unusual to consider Eastern women as a down-trodden poor-spirited race, and yet cases are numerous in which they have been the actual rulers, whilst fathers, husbands, and sons were of small account. Their masculine character has been exemplified of late in the tragedy of Jhansee, where, it may be remembered, numbers of our countrymen were slaughtered by the widow of the Raja, at whose death we took possession of the country, refusing to sanction an adopted heir, and thereby depriving her of rule and territory. This lady threw herself heart and soul into the rebellion, and died fighting against us on horseback, in the rebel ranks.

Raj Baee, the heroine of my present story, was a woman of a like masculine and determined character. At the time of the occurrences I am about to relate, she had been regent of her country, the Principality of Wudwan, in the Guzerat peninsula, some thirty years, during which time, according to public rumour, she had made away with successively her father-in-law, husband, and a son, as each interfered with her management more than she approved. Providence had now given her—or she had recently introduced—an infant successor, of which Goelwao, the young widow of the late Raja, over whom his mother supposed herself to have the most interest, was, or was proclaimed to be, the parent; for the male species, though to Raj Baee's view entirely useless in itself, was still necessary as a means of power—a sort of constable's staff without which her jurisdiction would not have been acknowledged, but the claim of some male heir set up instead.

Having related the dark crimes attributed to the old lady—let us charitably hope without sufficient foundation—it is but justice to her to state that her country was well-governed and in a flourishing condition.

Raj Baee was now nearly seventy years old, and having latterly pondered more and more on the prospects of another world, was troubled with compunctions of conscience for her doings in this. Whereupon, after much demur, and taking ghostly counsel, she resolved to wash away her sins by a pilgrimage to a celebrated shrine at a considerable distance from the country. As this would detain her long from home, she made arrangements for the administration by appointing Goelwao regent *ad interim*; after which, all being settled, and an auspicious day for departure duly calculated by the Brahmins, she set forth with a large retinue, and was for a while lost to the world.

Meanwhile, Goelwao tasted the sweets of power, and while doing so she very naturally began to reflect, that as mother of the young Raja, she had as much right to govern in his name as the grandmother. Possessing an equal share of spirit, she forthwith began a series of intrigues, tending to secure the adherence of many who were in a position to help her to retain power when her mother-in-law should again make her appearance.

Matters went forward smoothly and successfully, and when the old queen, having accomplished her pilgrimage and returned home, was desirous of entering her capital, she was quietly informed that the stars were unfavourable, and that she had better wait a little outside.

The old lady was not famed for patience; nevertheless, she waited till her small stock of it was exhausted, and then attempted to enter the town, but found the gates closed, and the guard deaf to her indignant remonstrances. A parley next took place between the two ladies, in which the older upbraided the younger with treachery, and the younger replied, that the good old lady could not do better at her time of life than continue to devote herself to spiritual affairs, that she might thereby gain the full benefit conferred by pilgrimage to the holy shrine, leaving to younger shoulders the burden of the troubled cares of this world. But Raj Baee failed to see the force of the argument; frustrated, and boiling with indignation, she bent her steps towards Rajcote, there to lay her grievances before the British authority. Being a wealthy dame, she took care to bring with her abundance of golden reasons for propitiating all amenable to a species of logic to which, it must be confessed, our native subordinates are not more insensible than many of the electors of our own boroughs. But her utmost efforts failed to do more than induce the Political Agent, the late Sir John Pollard Willoughby, to issue an attachment upon the State, that is, to place a functionary in charge of its management until some means of adjustment could be devised between the two belligerent parties. This species of sequestration leaves everything *in statu quo*. Goelwao therefore being actually in power, and having possession of the young Raja, had nine parts of the law in her favour.

Every attempt to arrange the dispute by arbitration or otherwise failed, as did also the old Queen's patience, and she determined to take the law into her own hands. Whether with or without the co-operation of the native officials of the agency, she contrived to gain over the native functionary acting for the British Government at Wudwan, to

C

secure some of the nobles of the country, and raise a body of mercenaries, thousands of whom can readily be obtained to cut one another's throats at a few shillings a head. All arrangements being completed, she left Rajcote, and took the field; mounted on horseback at the head of her troops, and attended by some of the chiefs, she once more presented herself at the gateway of Wudwan, this time in full hope of admittance. But some of the garrison, not let into the secret, or not sufficiently bribed, opened fire upon her, and a chief fell dead at her side. Nothing daunted, the plucky old lady rushed on, trusting to her star and to the success of her previous arrangements ; and not in vain, for the guard opened the gates to her, and she effected a triumphant entry into the town. There the obsequious sequestration officer had contrived to get possession of the person of the young Raja, whom he now made over to her, and thereby at once secured her control over the people. Outwitted and checkmated, Goelwao found herself compelled to beat a retreat, and in her turn besieged the British authority with the tale of her woes and with claims for restitution of what she considered her rights.

The above is a fair sample of many of the cases that repeatedly come before the Political authorities of India, in the settlement whereof but feeble assistance can be gained from all the works on international or any other written law. On one side it could be urged that power had been surreptitiously gained through a breach of faith ; on the other, that that power was the legitimate right of the mother rather than of the grandmother of the young prince. To this was answered that the grandmother had ruled, and ruled well, during thirty years, with the approbation of the leading men of the country, without whose consent, and foremost without that of the British Government, first obtained and deliberately expressed, no such change of regent should have been made, and especially not by stealth in the manner done. The mother rejoined that the consent of many of the leading nobles had been given her; that her mother-in-law was of an age fast unfitting her for public duties, of which her voluntary surrender of

the reins of government, to go on a distant pilgrimage, was a tacit admission ; that she took possession of the regency in the natural course of events,
without any necessity to do more than report the
fact for the information of the protecting government which had sanctioned the measure ; that she
had been in possession under the ægis of that
Government when forcibly dispossessed ; and that
the least that could be done was to restore her to
the same position pending the adjustment of the
dispute, unless the British Government allowed
force rather than justice to be the rule of right.

It is easy to perceive the delicate nature of such
transactions, and the difficulty of doing justice in
them. In the present case, apart from the danger
of establishing a precedent in favour of parties
taking the law into their own hands, more especially pending reference to Government on the
merits of the case, there were more reasons for
confirming the grandmother in the regency than
for ejecting her in favour of the mother, an unknown, untried person. These reasons prevailed
with the controlling authority, and the matter was

settled by a moderate fine on the grandmother, who was permitted to retain rule, and a maintenance was allotted to the mother.

This decision is to be regretted in its general effect on the country at large, as it formed an evil example for every aspirant to power, instances of which will appear in the following chapters. The true policy would have been to appoint a well-selected regency, setting both ladies on one side, and to rescue the young prince from the condition in which these were purposely keeping him, in order to prolong their own rule. To exercise interference only to keep things still, till they become rotten, is unworthy of our nation.

CHAPTER III.

PLOTS AND COUNTERPLOTS.

THE Raja[1] of Limree, a small Rajpoot state
adjoining that of Wudwan, in Kattywar,
died in 1837 at the age of eighteen, leaving three
young widows. His minister, Nuthoo Mehta by
name, was at the time in confinement at the
British Agency[2] on a charge of connivance in a
gang robbery that had occurred in his territory.
Great was the consternation in the little state at
the prospect of a change of dynasty, for the Raja
died without issue, and apparently without hope of
any. A conclave of the dowager queens met to

[1] Thakoor, *lit.* the Lord, is the more correct appellation of these
petty chiefs ; but this name being unfamiliar to English ears, I use
the term better known and which is also occasionally applied to them.
The same may be said of their Ranees, who should strictly speaking
be called Baee, *lit.* the Lady.

[2] I am sorry to say, an unjustifiable measure.

deliberate on the course to be pursued in this
emergency: they had hostile interests, each wishing the succession to be in the line where her influence prevailed. The sage old minister, Nuthoo
Mehta, a man highly respected for wisdom, tact,
and good temper, wrote to counsel a child being
placed in the lap of one of the young widows,
approved of by the majority, and possessing the
most influential connections. He had employed
his time whilst under restraint in making matters
smooth at the Agency; a douceur of a lakh of
rupees (10,000*l.*) was promised as a nuzzerana[1]
for the new Political Agent, Mr. E——, to his
moonshee acting chief native functionary, a very
able fellow, and high in his master's confidence,
named Lutf Ali; and when at last the gang
robbery charge proved a mare's nest, Nuthoo
Mehta was released from confinement, and allowed

[1] It may be as well to explain for English readers that *nuzzerana*
means the present given by Indian usage to the paramount power on
the accession of an heir to the gadee, a species of succession tax
which under British rule had not been enforced. We have of late
years preferred succeeding to the State ourselves when it suited our
purpose, a policy wisely disowned in the Queen's proclamation on
assuming the direct government of India.

to return to his country. He had arranged before-hand by correspondence with the ladies for the due succession of a selected infant. On reaching home, he sent half of the money promised in hard cash, with some of the Durbar jewels and gold orna-ments, to a neighbouring banker, agreed on between himself and Lutf Ali as the go-between in this transaction. The nuzzerana was to assume the shape of a loan from the said banker to Mr. E——, and was entered in his books accordingly.

Unfortunately for the smooth current of the plot, this abstraction of Durbar wealth was reported to head-quarters by Munguljee, the native officer placed in charge of the district, on the demise of the Raja, whereupon, however, he was removed, and a successor sent charged not to interfere with Durbar arrangements. Munguljee returned to Rajcote, the seat of the British Agency, envenomed against all who had caused his dismissal, and pre-pared to join anyone who would help to gratify his revenge. This he had perhaps previously found in a nephew of the late Raja, by name Akhabhaee, who, failing issue, was heir to the gadee,[1] and who now, both personally and through numerous friends in neighbouring states, was besieging the Agency with applications for attention to his claim. He and Munguljee united interests, and he was loud in his assertions that the latter's successor was a mere tool of the Durbar, during whose control no chance of preventing surreptitious procedure existed. These assertions were coldly received, and in despair of obtaining any effectual measures for securing his interests in the state, he proceeded to take the law into his own hands, and to raise troops, a course so recently followed with success in the adjoining Wudwan principality.

At this stage of the proceedings I became involved in the affair. Mr. E——, falling ill, was obliged to leave for one of the sanatariums of the country, and made over charge of the current work of his office to me, with directions to seize the troublesome aspirant to the gadee, and place him in confinement unless or until he should offer good

---

[1] Throne, literally cushion, but the English word is too grand a title for a petty principality.

securities for preserving the peace. From this time my native assistant became a prominent man in the drama, and secretly allied himself to Akhabhaee or rather to a third party yet to be mentioned, who made Akhabhaee their tool. It is needless to say that the representations of the latter were duly conveyed to the proper authority, with an intimation that as we were preventing him from acting for himself we were bound to see that justice was done him. Valid securities having been tendered, he was released from restraint, and thus for a while matters remained *in statu quo.*

But now a 'change came o'er the spirit of the scene,' at its principal theatre of Limree. One of the three young widows was declared to be with child, to the discomfiture of three out of the four dowager Ranees who had looked to perpetuate their power by the simpler process of placing an infant in the lap, as it is termed, of that widow who was under their influence, according to the plan arranged with Nuthoo Mehta. Great was the disgust of the aged trio, and, whether really disbelieving the allegation, or resolved at all cost to carry out the original design, they became at daggers drawn with the fourth dowager, who alone resolutely maintained the changed issue. This lady was the mother of the deceased Raja, and as such held the greater power in the Durbar. From the first she had only reluctantly joined in Nuthoo Mehta's scheme, and the old man finding that in spite of his tact the family feud was too much for him, thought it wisest to support her at this juncture. He was able to do so with considerable effect, for the apparent acceptance of the nuzzerana and the exchange of the obnoxious functionary for one more amenable to the Durbar, rendered his position very different to what it had been when in confinement.

Meanwhile Akhabhaee's party rapidly increased both within and without the State; nearly the whole of the bhayad[1] or nobles, that is, those connected by blood with the reigning family, joined it. These chiefs held large possessions of their own, the endowment of former rajas, and many of them were independent save the fealty paid of

---

[1] *Lit.* Brotherhood.

their own will and pleasure to the head of their family. To this party the three disappointed dowagers now turned, and heedless of the Napoleonic maxim concerning *linge sale*, gave up the correspondence between themselves and Nuthoo Mehta relating to the original plot. As the last letter was dated between two and three months after the Raja's death, it markedly strengthened Akhabhaee's claim, and seemed fatal to the hopes of the Durbar.

Limree, as a Rajpoot principality, in common with some others springing from the founder of the race whose descendants still reigned at Drangadra, cherished an old ceremony, the only sign left of its former power over its offshoots. The installation of one of these on the gadee was not considered complete without the attendance of the head of the tribe, or of his eldest son, to impress on his forehead in blood with a pricked finger, the central mark, called *tilla*, Hindoos so carefully paint afresh after their morning devotions. This family therefore bestirred itself on the question of the succession, and communicated to the British

Agency its willingness for the ladies of its house to be employed in testing the allegation of pregnancy set up.

Of all the intrigues alluded to, I was profoundly ignorant until the departure of my chief, when, as the senior assistant was absent, I became in a measure responsible, if not for the due administration of the affairs of the province, at least that nothing should transpire unreported affecting its interests and the character of our Government. Unknown to me, secret interviews had taken place between my native assistant, the dismissed Munguljee, and Deosee, a leading character at the capital, formerly much employed in public business, and still possessing influence.

It will be as well here to give a description of my assistant, Madhow Rao. He was an elderly Brahmin who had been educated at the court of the Peishwa, and there initiated in all the duplicity that was considered statesmanship. When his master fell he pursued his fortunes elsewhere, ending in the position he occupied under me. He was a man of great intelligence, full of much useful local knowledge, bland and courteous in his manners yet withal of a frank and open address.

Deosee was a colleague in every way fitted to join or cope with him; of mature age, possessing both Indian and English experience, on visiting and friendly terms with the European gentry, of great reputed wealth (some 30,000*l.* were in deposit at the Agency pending the adjustment of one of his disputes), subtle, plausible, and well mannered.

Munguljee was of an inferior stamp; he loved to work like a mole underground, and it was difficult to judge of the extent of his abilities.

These three met together in secret conclave. The fact I did not know till long afterwards; the purport was never disclosed: I can only judge therefore by the fruits. First, my man broke ground on a petition presented by Akhabhaee, complaining that the Government officer in charge of the district was a tool in the hands of the Durbar, openly supporting it, and refusing to let any of his people into the place, and declaring that there could be no doubt of preparations being in progress for the introduction of a spurious child as heir; and that as the British Government had tied his hands, he claimed that justice should be done him.

By the conversation that ensued upon this petition Madhow Rao was able to discover to what extent I might be depended upon, if his previous experience of my character left him any room for doubt. It is needless to state what took place between my chief and myself consequent on the above. The former, though at a distance, still held control of the general affairs of the province, whilst I was left at head-quarters transacting current work.

Shortly after receipt of this petition, Deosee paid me a visit. After the usual preliminaries, he said the main object of his call was to let me know, for Mr. E——'s information, as he was unable from lameness to travel all that distance himself, of the extraordinary reports prevailing in the town injurious to that gentleman's character, to wit, that a cart laden with rupees had been sent by the Limree Durbar into the town, and the next morning conveyed to the Agency treasury; and it

was in everybody's mouth that this was the money
sent as an equivalent for being permitted to keep
the reins of power in their own hands. He did
not credit this rumour himself, but it was so widely
circulated, that he thought it right to let Mr. E——
know, as he was well aware that the thing was
entirely opposed to British sense of propriety and
usage.

I duly conveyed this message, and the correspondence that ensued ended in my being directed
to proceed to Limree to make enquiries as to the
prospect or otherwise of direct succession, and as
to whether the money in question, which had
actually reached the capital in the way mentioned,
had been supplied by the Limree Durbar or not.
Madhow Rao was not allowed to accompany me,
but another sent in his stead. I accordingly proceeded to the spot, and the Drangadra family was
requested to join me there to assist in my enquiry.

The difficulty of such an enquiry it is impossible
for the uninitiated to realise. No male, not even
a brother after childhood, can see a young Raj-
pootnee of rank ; consequently, facts can only be

elicited through intermediate channels, at second hand, and with the knowledge that all concerned are more or less infected by that indifference to truth arising from the Eastern maxim that speech is given to man exclusively for his own benefit, an idea unhappily rather too prevalent even in the West.

Some time elapsed before the arrival of the Drangadra Ranees ; and during this interval I took measures for assembling a matron punchayut, that is, a committee of ladies, from amongst the principal people of the country, some named by the Durbar, others by Akhabhaee, to be in readiness to meet them ; at the same time pursuing my enquiry into the alleged bribe given to my chief for conniving at the introduction of a spurious heir. The proof became too apparent of the money having actually issued from the Limree Durbar, for Munguljee, when in power, had kept so keen a lookout, and gathered so many threads of the plot, that though the deed took place with every precaution, in the dead of night, it could not be effectually concealed.

D

The investigation by the ladies was long postponed under various pleas. What with unlucky
days of the calendar, or superstitious causes assigned by one or other of the parties concerned, it
really seemed as though it never would come off;
and as the chief delay was caused by the Durbar,
the reasons for disbelieving the likelihood of a
direct heir increased in strength. Unfortunately,
during all this time, Mr. E—— or his moonshee
corresponded directly with the Durbar instead of
through me, which had a most prejudicial effect on
my endeavours to convince them of my impar-
tiality; and this was rendered still more difficult by
the trial then going on at the neighbouring station
of Ahmedabad of the judge of the district, Mr.
Grant, by a commission which called on me to
examine the Limree minister, Nuthoo Mehta, on
matter pertaining thereto, the judge's assistant,
Mr. W. E. Frere, having been directed to pro-
secute.[1]

[1] An invidious duty to exact and impolitic to require from any assistant. In all such cases, happily rare, a special officer, unconnected
with the department, should be selected for the duty, that of the
assistant being limited to giving the information he possesses.

At last report was made to me that the claim was fictitious ; at the same time, however, the husband of one of the jury informed me that his wife was very strongly of an opposite opinion, but as he was a relation of the young would-be mother, his wife's verdict had but little weight. This embroglio was duly reported, and, as I had placed an intelligent man in charge of the town in supercession of Munguljee's inefficient successor, besides employing other means to arrive at the true state of affairs, I did not altogether despair of solving it, although it appeared all but impossible the Ranee should be really with child.

It was the usage in that part of India, on visiting the capital of any native state, for its Durbar to supply milk, firewood, and hay from their own dairy and preserves, and the attempts on the part of Europeans to break through this custom had been given up in consequence of the offence caused by non-acceptance. The feeling would have been as though an English traveller, after partaking of the hospitality of any gentleman, were to ask to be allowed to pay for his dinner, or were to buy his own food and have it cooked in his host's kitchen. Being anxious to stand well with the Durbar, and to give them no cause for suspecting I was their enemy, I permitted them to send the above-named supplies, although I received warning from different quarters, some anonymous, that under the very peculiar position I then occupied at Limree it behoved me to be careful against poison. I had hardly time to make up my mind what course to pursue with reference to this advice, when one morning, immediately after breakfast, I became deadly ill with vomiting and other choleraic symptoms; happily, the first was so violent as to get rid of everything I had taken. No medical man was within hail, and I remained exceedingly ill for some days. On afterwards mentioning my symptoms to the Agency doctor, he gave it as his opinion that I had probably been poisoned, and owed my life to its not having been taken into the system. Whatever was the real fact, I took good care to drink no more Durbar milk, but, in the absence of proof, thought it wiser to keep silent as to the cause.

Shortly after this, Mr. E—— suddenly resolved to come to the scene of action, bringing his lady with him, over-ruling my representation, that should the claim of the Durbar prove valid, the fact of a large sum of money having been paid with the view of gaining his consent to a spurious heir, would invalidate anything he himself might do, however ignorant he might have been of the source whence the money was derived. I could not prevent his coming, but he repaid through me, by an order on a Baroda banker, the amount of the money proved to have come from the Durbar; and I took good care in delivering this order in a ceremonial interview, that the fact should be publicly known, with due admonitions as to the folly of attempting to bribe a British functionary; stating at the same time that all the harsh usage that might possibly be necessary to test their claim, must be attributed to their own acts which threw such doubt upon it.

On Mr. E——'s arrival serious were the consultations between us, and it was at length decided that a letter should be written inviting the Ranees to visit Mrs. E——, which was acceded to, and they accordingly attended on the following night.

The splendid suite of tents of the Agency gave ample accommodation for numbers, and permitted of arrangements for privacy required by Rajpoot etiquette. The medical officer, Dr. Graham, had accompanied his chief. The ladies assembled in an inner tent, and after a while, thence issued a few lines in pencil to say that two of the young Ranees would certainly soon become mothers, one of them before long. This was about seven months after the Raja's death. On this Mr. E—— became sensible that with such a mass of direct and circumstantial evidence to the contrary, it would be improper to throw the whole onus of proof on his wife's testimony alone, and the Ranees were therefore informed that under the peculiar circumstances they must allow themselves to be seen by the Agency surgeon. The reply to this was that so serious a matter required time for deliberation before they could consent.

A difficulty had now to be provided for, to wit, the possibility if not probability of other parties having been, and continuing to be, passed off as the young queens, to meet which it was decided to invite on the occasion of the second examination the Drangadra Ranees and the three objecting mothers-in-law. The Durbar consented to this ordeal, as did also the Dowagers, and the Drangadra ladies sent their midwife in their stead. At this meeting, which took place again at night, Mr. E—— and I made arrangements for satisfying ourselves on the subject, unperceived. No doubt on our minds was left, and such, of course, was the surgeon's report, although the old Dowagers and the Drangadra deputy vehemently maintained the contrary, in spite of his efforts to convince them. It was a decided case of *tant pis pour les faits*, for the credit of the British Government would have stood much higher with the people had Mr. E—— been able to prove that nothing had been gained by the attempt to bribe him. It was evident that there had been deep counter-plotting based on the original plot of the Durbar, and that almost every one had been gained over to what seemed to be the winning side. The heir apparent could of course offer much heavier bribes than those who merely wanted to retain the power they held, and nothing daunted by this last examination, Akhabhaee's party declared the whole thing a delusion of the senses attributable to magic.

The necessity of removing as far as possible all public disbelief in the real facts, as well as to guard against the substitution of a male for a female child in case of the birth of the latter, was made known to the Durbar, and the Ranees were required to take up their abode, as a temporary measure, in a spacious mansion apart from other houses, with walled courts and gateway, there to await the issue of events. Windows accessible from without were barred, and a guard of regular troops under a British officer was placed in charge of the premises with several sentries all round and patrols every hour outside. In addition to these external precautions, the dowagers were requested personally to examine all their female attendants, who to the number of thirty or forty followed their mistresses, and to exclude from them any whose condition might be such as to complicate matters, which they did, and rejected three.

With all these precautions we trusted that the public mind would be convinced of the justice of the British Government, notwithstanding the unfortunate opening of the suit. The diverse parties brought together for adjudication of the knotty question went each their way, and I was left to await the *dénoûment* with a force to keep the peace as well as to guard the ladies. Dr. Graham was to vaccinate in the neighbourhood, so as to be within call in case of being further required. Party spirit for the moment seemed suppressed, but it was only resting to gather strength if further contest were needed—a lull between blasts of the cyclone blowing from the opposite quarters of plot and counterplot.

CHAPTER IV.

PLOTS AND COUNTERPLOTS—*concluded.*

SOME two months passed away, when one evening Dr. Graham came across country, on his
riding camel, to my tent, to enquire how things
were going on, and whether he could be of any use.
He passed the night on a sofa, intending to leave in
the early morning, but long before dawn we were
aroused by a Havildar (i.e. sergeant) of the guard
reporting that the Ranee was in labour.

'Well,' said I to my friend, 'it's lucky you
dropped in upon me at this crisis; but let us
hope it will be a girl, for if a boy they'll swear you
brought him with you in your saddle-bags.'

The first thing to be done was to summon the
Dowager Ranees, and some of Akhabhaee's trusted
adherents, to attend and bear witness of the result,
whatever it might be. We then rode into the town,

and sat at the gateway of the temporary palace where the guard was stationed, waiting for the expectant witnesses. Ere long we heard a shout which from its joyous tone put an end to Akhabhaee's hopes, and some of his fierce followers began to scowl at me savagely, for they suspected deceit. The gateway was now thrown open, and we entered the precincts. In a few minutes more the future ruler of the country was brought before us, unwashed and undressed, and what I suppose Mrs. Gamp would deem very untidy ; he was anything but a beautiful object except to Durbar eyes, that rejoiced in his sex as much as I deplored it.

Meanwhile the Dowagers delayed to come ; indeed, at first they had sent a message refusing to do so, but subsequently they yielded to the urgent remonstrance that their absence would prevent them satisfying themselves and others by personal observation of what might be destined for their country. The doctor pronounced all to be *en régle* as to the birth, and with his consent I refused to allow anything to be done till they had seen the child, thus bringing on myself loud and deep reproaches from the Durbar party, who upbraided me with risking the infant's life, and were hardly to be appeased by Dr. Graham's repeated assurance that there was no danger.

At length the dowagers arrived, and all was open for their inspection. I had not at that time become sufficiently hardened to native intrigue to hear without astonishment their exclamation that the child was not newly born, and, when after giving needful orders, Dr. Graham and myself left the place, I had the satisfaction, as a reward for all my pains to do justice to this people, to hear the ladies, as they drove away in their bullock carriages, exclaim on the dishonour I had brought on a Rajpoot throne by smuggling in some coolie's child to place on it. By this time a large crowd had assembled round the building, and the day had just dawned sufficiently to let me perceive the angry faces of many of the lookers-on, some of whom half drew their swords, thrusting them back again into the scabbards with vehement gestures.

We rode quickly to my tent, for I was glad to be away from the throng, and there over hot coffee and cigars we meditated on the vanity of human aspirations, and on the difficulty of getting partisans to believe anything against their will. The existence of a deep conspiracy, that previously I had banished from my thoughts, whenever the suspicion of it came across me, now returned strongly to my mind. How, thought I, could these ladies disbelieve the evidence of their senses when their idea of magic could no longer delude them, and how was it likely that they would have dared to outface the truth unless prompted and supported by powerful parties. Whilst cogitating these things, I received from them a letter, demanding an interview, remarkably well written, and in a handwriting that no one about me recognised. The interview was duly arranged, with curtains stretched across the tent, behind which the ladies and their female followers installed themselves ; a large gathering of Akhabhaee's party were also present. I give a portion of the conversation that ensued.

Ranees. 'We have come to ascertain what steps you intend to pursue relative to our throne.'

Self. 'Nothing but what is customary on the birth of an heir.'

Ranees. 'You do not really mean to tell us that

you consider the thing you showed us this morning to be our heir.'

Self. ' I am at a loss to know what you mean ; do you doubt the evidence of your senses ? '

Ranees. 'Not at all ; the child you showed us was at least two or three days old. We thought that you merely wanted to avoid a scandal, and let off the guilty parties as easily as possible consistent with the rights of our family ; but we wish positively to know what you are going to do, that we may take care that those rights should be maintained.'

Self. 'The British Government will uphold those rights ; and I am here, as its agent, to see that they are not sacrificed either by fraud on one side or by lying and conspiracy on the other.'

I then referred to proofs of recent birth which they had seen with their own eyes, reminded them that I had risked bad consequences by refusing to allow these to be removed till they were present ; that they were well aware how carefully the young Ranees had been guarded, not only by disciplined soldiers but by as many adherents of the opposite party as chose to watch or move round the place; that no vessel of any description had been permitted to enter without examination; that they themselves had previously examined the premises, and that all whom they objected to had been excluded.

To all which the old ladies replied that, how the child got in they could not tell, but that it had been smuggled in there was no doubt; that they knew better than I what a new-born child was, and that the proofs I alluded to were fictitiously got up, entering into details how this could have been done which fairly astonished me.

Certainly all this was a lesson in the school of native politics, for I had not previously conceived the depths of depravity to which intrigue would stoop. I informed them that I considered them guilty of treason to their own liege suzerain, and that I should not interfere with the right of the Durbar to place them in a position where they could do no further mischief, as parties in a conspiracy against those rights.

So ended my interview with the ladies. Akhab-haee and his party were dismissed with a brief summary of all that had been done to secure justice to their cause, and a warning against factious opposition.

The original plot of the Durbar had now been sifted, and they had undergone the pains and penalties of their attempt to purchase British justice. But all was not yet at peace. The disappointed party, instead of bending to the will of Providence, on being satisfied that every just measure had been taken to secure their rights, were resolved to obtain their ends by foul means when all fair ones had failed. It was evident that the lull during the imprisonment of the young Ranees had been caused by the hope that a female child might be born, but that in case of adverse issue they had secretly combined to deny it, basing their hopes on the existing proof that a spurious issue had at first been contemplated, and on the doubt which might be thrown on any decision by the local authority that had weakened itself by taking money from the Durbar. In this view it became necessary to them to charge my chief and myself, including of course all co-operating with us, with guilty connivance in the Durbar intrigue, and to make out that the imprisonment was merely a blind for the more effectually carrying it through. I ascertained that the stranger alluded to as writing the dowager Ranees' letter to me had been for some days their principal adviser, and closeted with the leading men of the adverse party.

On the dowagers being confined to their quarters by the Durbar, and placed under surveillance, this stranger disappeared as suddenly as he had come, but I was able to find out that he was a native lawyer of Ahmedabad, and to trace a connection between him and a person residing there who had been until very lately the leading native functionary in Kattywar, but had been suspended from office by Mr. E—— on charges of bribery, and was there awaiting the decision of Government on his case. This man, from his position, abilities, and long connection with the people, had greater influence over them than any other single individual ; and it appeared, therefore, pretty plain that he was taking advantage of the storm to bring his own bark back into harbour by turning the tables on his

E

opponent. Be this as it may, a master hand concealed from view evidently guided the conspiracy, for none other could have succeeded in welding together so much diverse material in the effectual way in which this plot was carried through.

One chief part of it had been to get possession of the person of the young Ranee on the plea of testing the claim set up on her behalf, which the usages of the Rajpoot community threw such vast difficulty in the way of doing except through female evidence ; and, after the spirit shown in this history it is evident that had they succeeded I should have been made an innocent accomplice in the crime of murder, while simply executing my duty.

It behoved me now to trace the ramifications of this intrigue, but the secrecy and prudence with which it had been conducted defied nearly all my attempts. Enough, however, was discovered to satisfy Government of its existence, and to give grounds for the punishment of some of those concerned, amongst others of my own assistant. It was of course impossible for Mr. E——, without taking the onus of the bribery transaction on himself, to retain Lutf Ali in public employ, and he was therefore sent away from the province.[1]

The discontented chiefs deputed several of their number to Bombay, armed with petitions and statements of grievances blackening my character in no sparing terms, which everybody was invited to read. Had the links in the chain of evidence establishing the birth of an heir not been so firmly riveted together, it is probable that they would have succeeded in their enterprise, but owing to the precautions taken, no room was left for doubt, and the combined ingenuity of all the intriguers, however directed, was exercised in vain. Government could not give them the redress they sought, and the young Prince was confirmed on the Gadee.

Thus ends the history of this singular exhibition of the difficulties of an Indian succession case. But before finally quitting the subject I will mention an anecdote told me by Mr. Le Geyt, the senior Magistrate of Police at Bombay, concerning these

[1] I ought, it appears, to have spelt this person's name Lutf Ullah, whose interesting autobiography, edited by Edward B. Eastwick, Esq., the present member for Penryn, I have read since the above was penned.

malcontents, who were, as above shown, foiled in their purpose. It forms an amusing illustration of the ignorance of men of rank and others in the interior, of the Government that controls them.

When a considerable time had passed without their having gained any of their objects, or obtained an interview with the authorities, a shrewd intriguer, one of the many who lie in wait to prey upon the ignorance of such people, got introduced, and offered to assist them. After feeling his way and ascertaining particulars, he told them the reason of their disappointment was, that they had not gone the proper way to work; it was of no use making offers of money until parties had been propitiated, for the English were a proud and wayward people, difficult for natives to understand, and who could only be managed according to their own usages. Chief among these was to do nothing without a good dinner, and when persons wished to get anything difficult done they gave a great feast and plenty of good wine; then, when the parties from whom aid was expected were drunk and jolly, and so put into good humour, the business of the evening was brought forward ; they must act in like manner with the officials from whom they expected anything. To get hold of the Governor was a very difficult matter, beyond the power of their friend, but he thought he could manage the secretaries for them if they were disposed to go to the expense.

It was at last settled that arrangements should be made for giving a dinner to the three leading secretaries, at which the chiefs should be in attendance, ready to be introduced at the auspicious moment. For the purely English reader it may be necessary for me to remark that they could not sit with Europeans at meals any more than the Jews would with the Gentiles, though I am happy to observe that some few of the upper classes are endeavouring to break through the prejudice.

A house was now procured in a fashionable quarter, dinner and wines ordered, and three European gentlemen, to personate the secretaries, were engaged to attend. These unhappy men were officers dismissed from the army and living by their wits; they were told that all that would be

required of them was a few civil words to certain
natives who would be introduced to them, to listen,
or at any rate to pretend to listen, to their tale, and
in reply to say that they would pay attention to
the case. Not being much in the way of enjoying
good things, these worthies revelled to their hearts'
content in champagne and other luxuries, and the
auspicious moment was not therefore long delayed.
With their turbans of gold brocade more than a
foot high, the chiefs were then solemnly introduced,
to make known their grievances, and were received
with an air of patronising dignity, and responded
to as laid down in the programme, after which they
retired, delighted with the interview, and satisfied
that the first stone was laid of Akhabhaee's throne.

Next day the intriguer presented himself to
congratulate them on their success, and to assure
them that, now the point of the wedge had been
driven in, they had but to follow it up to secure
their ends. How much more money he contrived
to victimize out of them besides a thousand rupees
advanced for the dinner, if told, I have forgotten;

but the bubble at last burst, and with it ends my story.[1]

[1] The difficulty of an Oriental understanding or appreciating the feeling of honour that leads an Englishman to scorn a bribe is well shown by a conversation I had with Nuthoo Mehta. We were on friendly terms, owing to his having proved himself one of the best arbitrators of the Province, for there being no Civil Courts, disputes and claims are generally adjusted by Punchayuts. 'How is it,' I asked, 'that one so renowned for sagacity as you are should not have known the British character better than to attempt to bribe the Political Agent?' 'Will you permit me to ask a question?' he replied. 'Certainly; as many as you please.' 'Well, then, tell me, if you did not come to India to make money, what did you come for?' I need not give my answer to this, nor to his next question—'What is the use of power if you do not profit by it?'

CHAPTER V.

SUCCESSION TROUBLES.

AFTER the foregoing history it will not be difficult to understand that of all the cases brought before the British Political authorities in India the most troublesome arise from disputed claims to succession on the death of the several Rajas and Chiefs—a difficulty often created and always enhanced by the practice of polygamy universally prevalent in that class, whether Hindoo or Mohammedan. Of the petty potentates, few have less than three or four wives, some of whom bring with them claims of superiority over the others in virtue of higher rank or caste, so that on a Raja's death it may happen that a younger son will have a prior claim to the elder. The mother of each adheres to the cause of her own child as the hunted tigress to her cubs, and it is often no easy matter for the Political Agent to decide between them.

On the occasion to which I am about to refer the sudden decease of the Nawab of Joonagur left three claimants to the throne—the eldest, in virtue of a written document, signed with the seal of state, formally acknowledging him as heir though he was not the Nawab's son. His mother had been wife to one of the chiefs of the country, but having great personal attractions, she had been induced by the Nawab to obtain a divorce and marry him—an arrangement she acquiesced in on the condition that her son was acknowledged heir to the throne.

The mother of the second claimant was of an inferior degree, not of noble blood; but after the Nawab had gained his object in securing the former wife, he had habitually treated the deed of succession alluded to as a dead letter, and associated the second claimant's name with his own in deeds of State, publicly proclaimed him heir, and treated him as such.

The third claimant was a child of four or five,

whose mother was of royal blood, and considered that her son had the best right to succeed in virtue thereof.

According to the loose usage of the country, something might be said in favour of the first, and still more of the youngest; but as the principal persons in the State then supported the cause of the second, and for other reasons in favour of his claim, needless to detail, he was acknowledged by the British Government as successor to the throne. He was a lad of about thirteen, very handsome, with engaging manners, intelligent beyond his years, and well worthy of the preference accorded him.[1] Though generally acknowledged by the people, the two disappointed mothers refused allegiance. So long as they remained quiet it was unnecessary for Government to interfere; but they secretly began to plot, surrounding themselves with armed mercenaries, and rendering it imperative on the administration of the country to take steps to preserve peace. The eldest queen first

---

[1] It is to be regretted that our Government did not take advantage of so good an opening for educating men to their responsibilities as was here afforded them, and pressed on their attention.

began this opposition, the younger apparently waiting the disposal of her case, perhaps secretly joining her; but as there was at this time no overt act on her part, she will not be alluded to again in this chapter.

Remonstrances and warnings producing no effect, I proceeded to Joonagur with a force sufficient to quell opposition should diplomacy fail. We encamped within the city walls, and after fruitless discussion with her agents I demanded an interview with the Ranee [1] herself. Captain Hutt, who commanded the troops, accompanied me, both to add weight to my injunctions and to survey the premises, which might possibly have to be attacked. We found them well suited for musketry defence, with many twists and turns where invaders might be taken in front and rear. Carefully observing everything that could be of use to us, we reached at last an inner room, where the Ranee's presence was announced behind a curtain that hid her from our view.

[1] Ranee is the Hindoo term for queen. The Mohammedans style her Begum when of the higher class of sovereigns, otherwise Baee, another Hindoo word, is the most appropriate title for both communities.

After the usual interchange of compliments, I fully explained the reasons for the rejection of her son's claim, and why the reigning prince had established his title. The lady heard me, and when I paused for her reply it came in no wavering tone ; with great ingenuity she supported her son's claim, and resolutely refused to give it up or to disband her followers. Argument failing, I was obliged to tell her that this state of things could not be permitted, that I had force enough with me to compel obedience, and that after giving over the affair to the military I could not be answerable for the consequences that might follow the storming of the place. All was in vain ; no persuasion could avail to shake the mother's determination. 'I care,' she said, 'for nothing but my son's rights, and for these I am ready to run all risks or sacrifice my life. Nothing shall induce me to give up his claim.'

The conference had lasted long, and further parley appearing hopeless, I drew out my watch, and solemnly warned the Ranee that I should wait only five minutes longer, after which I must make

over the whole business to the officer at my side.
The five minutes passed, and her resolution remained
unchanged. Then we rose slowly to go, inspecting
very minutely every step of the way, for it was important to see what positions it would be necessary
for the soldiers to take up after entrance was
effected. The way out was mostly lined with
matchlock men, their matches lighted for instant
service. This had rather an ugly look, as had also
their commander, whom I accosted. He and his
men, numbering about a hundred, were Arabs.
He had but one eye, the many deep scars on his
face showing how the other had been lost; and
small-pox had also left its traces on this charming
visage. He was armed to the teeth with pistols,
crease, dagger, and sword, all kept from jostling one
another by a huge shawl bound round his waist.
The following dialogue ensued between us :

'My friend,' I said, 'the Ranee has refused to
attend to the injunctions of Government, though
handsome terms of maintenance suited to her
dignity have been offered to her ; she has therefore
placed herself in the position of a rebel against

both her Government and mine, and those who aid
her in this course will incur the penalty of rebellion.
You must be aware that, however you may be able
to oppose your own sovereign, it is utterly impossible for you to prevail against the British Government, and opposition to the forces of either will
inevitably entail on you death in action or a
traitor's doom.   I therefore conjure you to disband
your men.   If you do so at once no harm or loss
shall accrue to you, for you shall be enlisted in the
service of the State, and all arrears of pay made
up.'

The Jemadar [1] replied, ' All that you say may be
very true, Sahib, but we Arabs look on the one
who pays us as our Dhuné,[2] and we pride ourselves
on being faithful to our salt.   When the Ranee
gives me an order I shall obey it.   I can't attend
to you.'

To this I replied that the lady's honour was safe

---

[1] Title of the commander of any small body, and may correspond
to Captain in the forces of Native States, though in our regular
Native Infantry rather to Ensign.

[2] The English language cannot give the full meaning.   *Dhuné*
implies owner, master, and lord paramount.

unless he persisted in supporting her in rebellion, and that by consenting to my terms he would save both her and himself.

'Talk to the Ranee,' he answered; 'it's no use speaking to me; I obey her orders only.'

Diplomacy had failed with these stubborn characters, and there was nothing left but to make the best of our way out of a hornets' nest. Captain Hutt, being in uniform, had his sword, but otherwise we were unarmed and entirely at their mercy.

The two princes, the elder about eighteen, the other two years younger, had accompanied us from their mother's apartment, as enjoined by Durbar etiquette; and now, as I mounted my horse, one seized my right and the other my left leg, exclaiming as they did so that I must not leave them, that they looked to me to uphold the just claim of the family, and so on, mingled with urgent expressions of hope and despair. The Arabs rushed out after their young masters and completely surrounded me. Here was a scene. Turning to my companion, who was not molested, I said, 'God knows how this may end. At present I am decidedly in what Yankees call a fix. You had better go off while you can, and lose no time in getting the troops ready for action. If I am killed or made prisoner, use your own discretion; if possible, I will join you soon.'

Perhaps it was fortunate those around me did not understand English, or he might have been stopped before my speech was done; but as it was he put spurs to his horse and galloped off to the force.

Left alone, I kept urging my horse forward, using meanwhile every persuasion to induce the princes to return to the house, appealing to their sense of dignity not to demean themselves by acting as grooms; but in vain, they would not leave my stirrup leathers nor the Arabs my bridle. It was evident they had not made up their minds how to act, and I took advantage of this indecision to push my horse on, and gradually gained ground.

Thus we went slowly forward, until on suddenly turning a corner we faced the encamping ground of the troops. Here drawn up in line were horse, foot, and artillery, and I pressed on to the centre front.

The ringing of the muskets as the men loaded and the glistening of the port fires of the guns acted somewhat as a shower-bath to cool the ardour of my troublesome escort; but they would not leave me, and I was their prisoner. Meanwhile Captain Hutt galloped up towards me, and I shouted to him that I hoped with prudent management we might still get through without bloodshed. 'I'll ply these fellows vigorously with talk,' I said, 'while you, as if executing a parade movement, file your men, ranks opened out, through this crowd, and let each man pinch out the match of the Arab near him, after which, as gently as possible, let them seize the matchlock, but on no account touch the side-arms unless driven to it by their using them.'[1]

The whole plan was admirably carried out. The Arabs found themselves prisoners before they well knew what our men were about, and were sent off under a strong guard, with the promise that if they behaved well they should be forgiven. Then

---

[1] Bloodshed has often been needlessly caused by the endeavour to deprive Arabs of their side-arms. The retention of them is a point of honour, and many will die rather than give them up.

F

addressing the princes still by my side, I said, 'See to what a condition your refusal to listen to my advice has brought you. I cannot let you go back in the degrading way you chose to come. You shall return as befits your position, on horseback, and with a suitable escort.'

This was soon arranged, and the officer in command had instructions to accompany the princes to the palace, and once inside to keep there. The few armed men remaining within were unequal to any opposition, and the guard of honour quietly became masters of the place. The Queen was detained prisoner until she furnished satisfactory security against any further disturbance of the peace, when she was released, and a suitable maintenance allotted to her. The rebellion being thus quietly suppressed, the force broke up, not, however, before many had been struck down by the fever prevalent at that time of year. Amongst those who fell victims was its commander, Captain Richard Hutt, an excellent officer, to whose skilful management and cordial co-operation much of the successful termination of the case was due.

What blood might not have been shed had the troops been under an officer unused to deal with natives, however well up in military routine, and knowing that his prospect of appearing in a gazette depended on 'a good butcher's bill.'

CHAPTER VI.

MORE SUCCESSION TROUBLES.

THOSE who have followed me thus far will remember that there was another claimant to the throne of Joonagur in the person of the youngest son of the deceased Nawab, whose mother rested the claim on the fact of her own higher rank. Some time after the troubles recorded had subsided, the intrigues of one or both dowagers raised considerable hostility to the reigning prince. One entire State, that of Mangrol, threw off its allegiance, and a discontented grassia, or land-holder, a Katty, Hursoor Wala by name, irritated by some infringement of his rights during the last reign, was tempted to raise the standard of revolt, and gathered around him some four score followers.

The determined disobedience of the rebel State to all the advice and injunctions of the agency forced me to represent to Government that no means of preserving the peace of the country remained without backing diplomacy by force, and this view being approved, I received permission to employ troops at my discretion. And further, on the military authorities afterwards ordering the artillery away from the province for its annual exercise at a distant station, Government, at my request, directed the Commander-in-chief not to remove it.

During this lull before the local storm, the great Afghanistan hurricane set in, regarding which the only orders I received were the instructions sent to all political authorities by Lord Auckland, then Governor-General, passed on for my guidance by the Government of Bombay, to the effect that, while exercising the utmost caution to keep clear of entanglement in any Political question, equal care was to be taken to avoid showing the white feather, and no steps should be retraced when the so doing might be attributed to weakness, and thereby encourage opposition.

Armed with the sanction of Government, I had

already warned the Mangrol Durbar that its obstinacy would be subdued by force if necessary, but that I was so unwilling to have recourse to it that I gave them yet a short time for consideration.

Meanwhile, Hursoor Wala and his men had taken up a position among the fastnesses of a jungle, known as the Geer, one mass of ridges and ravines, covered with low forest trees and bushes, about a hundred and fifty odd miles in circumference, where it would have been as difficult to find them as the proverbial needle in the bundle of hay. What added to the difficulty was the absence of water throughout nearly the whole region, which, however, prevented any lengthened sojourn therein of the rebels, and obliged them to get their needful supplies from friendly villages scattered round the borders.

The young Nawab was fortunate in possessing a minister both able and energetic, and Hubeeb Khan, for that was his name, had done his best to bring the rabble of the State army into something like order, though, with so many conflicting interests raging, it was difficult to know on whom to depend.

This force was employed to check the incursions of the rebels.

It was now that, whilst preparing for a march on Mangrol, I suddenly received information of a plot by which some of Hursoor Wala's men were to be admitted secretly into the city of Joonagur during a procession of the young Nawab, to take place on a certain state occasion a week later. Advantage was to be taken of a convenient opportunity during the customary *feu de joie,* or desultory firing, practised on such occasions, to shoot him. The people would naturally rally round the party whose succession to the Gadee would then remain undisputed.

I was at a week's distance by post from Bombay, therefore, if I moved at all in the matter, it behoved me to do so at once, without waiting for the Government reply to my despatch on the subject, nor did it occur to me as necessary, sanction for the employment of force having already been given, no counter-orders received, and the emergency plainly requiring it; for the Mangrol Durbar, the ambitious Ranee, and the Geer rebels were evidently acting in concert. The first had already come into collision with the Nawab's supporters within Mangrol, and after a struggle had succeeded in expelling its own Karbaree (minister) for his opposition to their rebellious tendencies. He, however, contrived to hold one gateway of the town, all the rest being in the hands of his opponents. From this insecure position urgent messages arrived from him for speedy support, failing which he must surrender or escape. Prompt action alone appeared the way to prevent anarchy and bloodshed, the end of which it was impossible to conjecture, and I accordingly took the field with all the troops that could be spared from cantonment duty; but a large number of irregulars had previously been despatched to guard the passes of the Geer, leaving open only one in which quarter were villages known to furnish the rebels with supplies. These villages Hubeeb Khan was endeavouring to bring under his control or failing that, active supervision; for all which purposes he had some two thousand of the Nawab's Sebundee or militia, and our plan was aided by some hundred Gaekwar horse, from the contingent stationed in the province under my orders.

Towards this quarter of the Geer we marched, and halted in its neighbourhood, knowing that the rebels must come out for supplies. Whilst thus encamped parties of the Nawab's Sebundee were, under cover of night, pushed up to the neighbourhood of these villages, and withdrawn before daybreak. They had orders to act according to any information they might receive during the night; to attack, if strong enough, or send to me for assistance.

During this interval my astonishment and disgust may be imagined on receiving from Government an express,[1] in reply to my report of the intended march, censuring me in the severest language for the rashness with which I had taken the field without waiting for sanction, which they therefore withheld, and ending by saying that, should this despatch reach me too late to prevent hostile operations, Government threw upon me the onus of all difficulties that might ensue, and, in case of success, would refuse me any credit.

---

[1] As the mail was carried by foot-runners the whole way, the term was little better than nominal.

Two courses were now before me ; one, to break up the force and return to cantonments, leaving the country to its fate ; the other, to persevere under shelter of the words *too late,* and take all risks upon myself, to say nothing of the possibility of being charged with murder by the relations of men killed in the conflict, and thus, as it were, proceeding with a halter round my neck.   Under the circumstances mentioned, it appeared to me that I ought to throw self entirely aside, and do only what was best for the public interests : on the one hand, to quench a triple firebrand, which I had every hope of doing ; on the other, to save myself from pains and penalties, and barely even that, for the Government might hereafter attribute all the convulsion that was certain to ensue, to my drawing back after having once begun.   I decided, therefore, on endorsing the despatch with ' too late,' and locking it safely up, lest other eyes should see it, and become paralysed.

Had the Nawab's government been sufficiently consolidated, I might have carried on the war with its aid alone, but the retreat of the regular troops at such a crisis would have been a temptation to his undisciplined soldiers, further disorganised by party feelings, to follow their own inclinations. The Joonagur factions were likely to be too strong for the young king unassisted. The Nagur Brahmins, who had lost power by his accession, secretly favoured the rival claims, and no other class in the whole Peninsula equalled this in influence both from superior attainments and power of combination. Moreover, Nagur Brahmins filled all the native departments of the Agency, and sympathised with their brethren at Joonagur, though of course endeavouring to conceal this from me. Added to which, the Nawab's mother, being of inferior rank to her rivals, had less weight with the upper classes of the country, and had weakened what she did possess by encouragement given to a favourite, a conceited upstart named Nuthoo Khan, who gave himself the airs of a grandeé, and was universally disliked. It was evident to me that Government were shaken by the Afghanistan tragedy then being enacted to such an extent as to make them magnify the comparative insignificance of that going forward nearer home, and also forget that the sanction previously granted had not been revoked, and that I was both literally and virtually carrying out the instructions sent for my guidance.

Happily, I had not long to wait before the plan of operations going forward bore fruit. A party of the rebels, including their fighting leader Bhoja Munganee, came forth from the Geer for information and supplies. Tidings were immediately conveyed by parties in the village gained over by Hubeeb Khan to his nearest outpost, the most trusty men being employed watching. These advanced in the darkness, and pounced on the insurgents, who, taken unawares, fled, leaving Bhoja Munganee and another man also of note. Entirely surrounded in one of the houses, and unable to escape, the two preferred death to surrender. In Bhoja Munganee's saddle-bags was found a recent letter from the rebels in the capital, denoting unity of design, though otherwise so guardedly worded as to be useless. His death took the sting from Hursoor Wala's revolt, for the latter, being incapable of guiding a movement, the party was kept together by the influence and ability of the other, who was known throughout the country as Hursoor Wala's sword. Had Bhoja lived, the troop might have been increased by hundreds at any time who would willingly have flocked to his standard.

Danger number one being thus overcome, the state of affairs at Mangrol next urgently demanded a remedy, for every day that decisive measures were postponed not only risked the destruction of the Nawab's faithful band there, but also hazarded a greater peril. The Mangrol State was under the widow of its chief as Regent, an elderly woman of determined character. She had sent agents to Bombay to besiege Government, or all they could get hold of there, to avert my threatened measures; and as, unfortunately, there was little difficulty by sufficient expenditure in obtaining access to the information recorded in the Secretariat, there was great probability of their having thus found out that these measures had not received the approval of Government. This information they could send by their own vessels to the port of Mangrol even quicker than by the post, and should it reach that place before I did, my authority would be held at naught, negotiations frustrated, and possibly the whole strength of the Durbar used to oppose force by force.

I proceeded, therefore, by rapid marches to Mangrol ; the portion of the Geer already described had lain in our route. On arrival no time was lost in requiring the attendance of competent parties to adjust the pending difficulties. After full discussion I dictated fair and honourable terms necessary to secure continued allegiance, and to shut out the causes that might interfere with it. The Durbar, while not absolutely declining these terms, sought to prolong the negotiations—the very thing that, for reasons given above, I was most anxious to prevent. I therefore gave them one hour to say Yes or No, and failing a decisive reply, the whole force at my disposal would, I assured them, attack the place. The hour passed, and no reply reached me.

This was one of the most anxious moments in my life, for I felt almost as if my own Government were fighting against me. The place was

strong, and, though I could get inside, there was
no knowing how street-fighting might end against
a resolute enemy. Yet it was impossible to recede,
and I ordered' the advance. For a while I was
under the painful impression that the Durbar must
have received from their agents the communication
by sea that I dreaded, as I fancied nothing else
could lead them to refuse the fair and most
equitable terms offered. But at the very last
moment I was stopped by a deputation from the
Durbar accepting these. terms, and thus the war
cloud passed away and a load of anxiety was
removed.

I need not enter into the details of how order
was restored to the place. Whilst negotiations
had been going on at Mangrol, news arrived of an
insurrection at Joonagur. The mother of the claimant to the Gadee, having, more or less secretly,
gathered together an armed force, whether stung
by disappointment at the overthrow of her plots,
the fall of one ally, and the approaching loss of
another, or in a fit of despair, now rose against the
remnant of the Nawab's troops in Joonagur, killed

their commander, and took up a strong position within the walls. The Nawab's power had nevertheless become, I thought, sufficiently consolidated to secure the fidelity of his own troops for any forcible measures that might still be necessary, and I broke up the field force, making, however, requisition on the officer commanding to halt at Joonagur, pending the issue of proceedings against the rebellious Ranee, conducted by Hubeeb Khan, with instructions to support him should he call for aid.

No time was lost in assaulting the lady's stronghold, which was carried with very little loss by an ingenious device of the minister. A line of low huts outside the inclosure abutted on the main wall of the building in which the Ranee had taken up her quarters. In these huts a body of men to act as sappers was introduced unobserved, eight pieces of artillery and the main part of the Nawab's forces being drawn up in front, and advantage was to be taken of this sham attack, which was purposely directed to frighten rather than damage, to force an entrance unperceived in the rear, through the walls, into the heart of the place. The manœuvre was entirely successful, the Ranee being taken by surprise, and the whole party captured with little bloodshed. And so the triple rebellion was crushed, and the regular troops returned to cantonments without having fired a shot.

Everything being thus happily adjusted, and the peace of the country restored, I had hoped that Government would have seen cause to modify their previous judgment of my proceeding, and allow me credit for what had been accomplished; but I hoped in vain, the Government contenting itself with expressing satisfaction at the restoration of order, but referring me to the former censure for the mode in which it had been effected.

My readers may perhaps be as surprised as I was at the opinion of the Court of Directors passed on receipt of the Bombay Government report on the subject, that Captain Jacob ought not to have employed troops without first obtaining leave, but that it was satisfactory to find that the Nawab's government was sufficiently consolidated to enable him to quell insurrection by his own resources,

Such was my reward ; and I had the further satisfaction of finding on my return to Rajcote that a
report that I had been bribed to support the
Nawab had been industriously circulated, and
considered by my raw assistants worthy of notice.
These officers had been temporarily employed
during the absence of others, and were but little
acquainted with the wiles and stratagems of native
politics.

It had been given out that the whole affair
was a treacherous plot and murder. I had some
trouble in tracing the libel to its source, and
even then, having suitable slime to live in, the
snake was but scotched ; for fourteen years afterwards, whilst engaged as Political Agent in Kutch,
on a joint commission with the Political Agent of
Kattywar, I had occasion to look up bygone
records, and to my astonishment and, I may say,
indignation, found a report on the subject of
Hursoor Wala's claims had been submitted to
Government shortly after I left the province, in
which the calumny about the death of Bhoja was
revived, the insurrection treated as nothing, Hur-

soor Wala made to appear an innocent victim of ill-treatment, as if he had not cut himself off from redress by taking the law into his own hands, and disturbing the public peace. After procedure of this kind, to concede such a person's claims is to offer a premium to insurrection. I, of course, took care to point out the inaccuracies of this document ; but the whole subject was dead and buried ; where I will allow it to lie, merely reverting to it to show the entanglements by which political officers in India are surrounded.

CHAPTER VII.

A VERY DISCURSIVE CHAPTER, SHOWING THE
DIFFICULTIES A POLITICAL OFFICER MAY BE
PLUNGED INTO WITHOUT FAULT OF HIS OWN,
AND WHAT GREAT EVENTS FROM LITTLE
CAUSES SPRING.

THE Guzerat Peninsula is now known by the name of Kattywar, about as correct a term as if England were called Yorkshire. Its native name, one that it has possessed from the earliest dawn of history, is Soorashtra, the land of the Sun; it also means the good or holy land. It is sacred in Hindoo estimation from having been the scene of Krishna's exploits and death, and hundreds of thousands of pilgrims come from all parts of India to visit its shrines. On its western coast stood the celebrated temple of Somnath, with which the episode

of the gates and Lord Ellenborough's famous proclamation have made the British public acquainted.

Whilst alluding to it I may remark that seldom
has an act been more misrepresented by contem-
porary writers. The whole Press of India seized
it as an opportunity for attacking a ruler who from
the haughty and imperious nature of his temper
had treated it, and with less reason the Civil Service also, with unjust contempt; and so the changes
were rung on the insult to Mohammedans, ignorance
of Hindoo feeling, encouragement to idolatry, and
so forth. As Committee-man I was in occasional
correspondence with the Secretary of our Geo-
graphical Society, Dr. Buist, then also Editor of
the 'Bombay Times,' one of the fiercest of Lord
Ellenborough's revilers, and being at that time in
control of the Province I told him that he had
been led astray by false information, in that I had
received a written request from the Nawab of
Joonagur, in whose territory the old and new
temples stood, and whose prime minister was Mohammedan, as was of course the Nawab himself, to
be allowed the honour of restoring the gates, and

that their advent was hailed by every Durbar in
the country in the light Lord Ellenborough intended, namely, as a proof that they were safe from
savage invaders from the north so long as India
was true to itself. But the animus prevailing at the
time was too strong to allow any counter-repre-
sentation to be heard, and mine passed unnoticed.

To return to my subject. The Peninsula became chiefly known to us by the inroads of the
tribe of Kattees, the inhabitants of the central
division or province, of which the Peninsula altogether possesses ten, eight belonging to Rajpoots of
diverse tribes, and one alone, Soruth, that had been
wrested from the Rajpoots, to the Mohammedan
dynasty of Joonagur. The Kattees trained a hardy
breed of horses and were expert riders, resembling
in their habits our border riders of old. The Rajpoots for the most part contented themselves with
their own internecine wars, and the whole Peninsula being a *terra incognita* to us, the less dignified
and less numerous Kattee tribe had the honour of
stamping their name, at least in English records,
on the whole country.

In 1805 Colonel Walker, Resident at Baroda, first established something like order throughout the land, and checked the savage incursions of the Mahratta hosts that annually laid it waste on the plea of levying tribute (the Mahratta Chowth) for the Peshwa and Gaekwar, by arrangements for paying certain sums regularly on one part, and abstaining from hostile incursions on the other, to which all parties consented. His name has deservedly been held in honour ever since, and his settlement deemed the Magna Charta of the country. As a straw shows the way of the wind, so the name of one tax levied by the Mahrattas, ' *dant ghusae,*' lit. teeth-grinding, may show their mode of dealing with the inhabitants. It was a cess imposed for every day's detention before payment of their demands, on the plea that they were then kept needlessly wearing away their teeth !

The Peninsula is, or was in my time, one of the best hunting-grounds of India for a large variety of game, from the lion down to the quail ; but as it is not my object to tell of sporting adventures, I refer to one only as an illustration of a trying position.

In the year 1842 my trackers had long been engaged in tracing to his lair a lion celebrated for his deeds of blood and for his colour, hence the black lion was a coveted prize. Information was at last brought that this wandering animal, whose thirty and forty miles of circuit a-day had so long harried my men, was settling down, and I was advised to encamp at a certain central spot about eighty miles from Rajcote, to be near at hand for the final *coup*. All seemed quiet at head-quarters, so I resolved on the venture. Placing spare horses, &c. &c. on the way, to go to and fro without loss of time, and sending on tents and all requisites, I sallied forth, travelling all night, and on reaching my ground received the report that my men felt sure in another day or two to mark him down where he would rest for the day. Thus on the tiptoe of expectation, my battery made ready, I was next morning surprised by the receipt of a despatch from my Assistant at head-quarters, in-forming me that a great calamity had fallen on the Agency. A man occasionally employed as a Mohsulee peon being kept longer than he liked from obtaining service, had entered the Agent's office, cut down the head accountant, and killed or wounded altogether seven persons before his bloody career was cut short by a bayonet-thrust from a sepoy of the guard. All was in confusion, and the writer puzzled how to act.

In this emergency it became necessary to sacrifice pleasure to duty; my guns were reluctantly restored to their cases, and all prepared for starting homewards, when to my further trial, a horseman came galloping in waving his turban: the black lion was marked down, his lair surrounded, and my trackers had sent the messenger to say, 'Come soon and you will be sure of him; all are watching till your arrival.' Alas! the spot was twelve miles away, and in an opposite direction to Rajcote. A whole day, even if one day sufficed for my noble enemy, must needs be spent in going, killing, and returning worn out with fatigue—how were eighty miles homewards over rough roads to be attempted! It was a trying moment, for I had spent much. money in bringing about this desirable object now within reach, yet was compelled to forego it because a man with a purely imaginary grievance had run a muck, thrown my whole establishment into disorder, and no one on the spot was capable of meeting the difficulty !

I never had again the opportunity of finding my lion, and I only hope that my bitter disappointment, equally felt by my trackers, and more or less shared in by the many who were gathered together for the occasion, may have had one good effect in showing them that their English rulers allow no temptation to make them swerve from the path of duty, for it is not often they find this the case with their own.

Before quitting the subject of sport, I must say a few words about the trackers. These men, called Puggees, or foot-tracers, rival what Cooper's novels tell us of the Red Indians. I have often followed them with astonishment, being unable to discern marks that satisfied them ; a bent twig is a sign-post, a dent in the ground a book wherein they will read size, age, sex, and time of day. I will give one of many proofs as a sample of their acumen.

In 1852 I was making the circuit of Kutch, and

halted at a little lake, which, being at a distance
from the capital, promised an abundant supply of
wild duck.   To my surprise I found that with all
my care I could not get within shot ; it was evident
they had been recently disturbed, and whilst skulk-
ing round behind the bushes, admiring the sagacity
with which the beautiful plumaged creatures mea-
sured the strength of powder, one of my shikarees
exclaimed, ' Here, sir, is the secret—see these foot-
marks ! '   From them he read the names of two
persons, master and man, and declared that they
must have been on this spot near a given hour the
previous day.   On my return some days afterwards
to head-quarters, I questioned my friend Lieut.
Newall about it, and it appeared that he had been
at the place the very day and hour named by my
shikaree.   This young officer, a bold and expert
rider and thorough sportsman, met a few years
afterwards with a sad accident—a rearing horse fell
back upon him, dislocating his spinal column, thus
cutting him off in the prime of life from the public
service in which his energy and ability gave promise of success.   Now, the upper part only of his

frame unparalysed, he soothes his misfortunes and amuses the public by works of fiction and the record of scenes of Indian life and sporting adventure.

But I must return to more serious subjects. The *amok* of the discontented sepoy led to what, without allusion to the opium-consuming habits of the nobles and gentry of the Peninsula, will be unintelligible. They do not smoke like the Chinese, but chew and drink it as a beverage, pounding and mixing it with water *ad lib.* No blood feud can be staunched, that is, agreement of peace sealed, without each man drinking this diluted laudanum from the palm of his enemy's right hand.

In 1822 our Government assumed direct control over the tributaries of the Peshwa and Gaekwar, and arrangements were made whereby the chiefs bound themselves to take the opium required for their several districts from the Government warehouse.

It was found that nearly all the opium previously consumed had been brought into the province from Malwa without a pass note, that is, without

payment of the regulated tax on export. Government agreed to give this opium to the chiefs at
cost price, including the tax, they agreeing to co-
operate in suppressing its illicit introduction. To
encourage them in this agreement they were to
receive two-thirds' value of all smuggled opium
that might be seized within their respective boun-
daries, one-third going to the informer and captors.

On my assuming control of the Province I found
that this agreement had become a dead letter;
scarcely any opium was taken from the warehouse,
smuggled opium everywhere in use, and of course
the cheaper the drug the more deleterious to the
population. I could get no help from the chiefs,
and whatever was done to intercept the illicit trade
had to be done by the Agency. Getting trace of a
consignment of smuggled opium, some of my police
followed and seized it when it had reached the
Jusdhun Talooka. The Kattee chief was a great
encourager of the contrabands, and had never kept
his engagement with Government; I felt it right,
therefore, to recommend that his claim to partici-
pation in the proceeds should be forfeited, on the

ground of his having broken the pact that assigned it to him. At the same time I sketched a
plan for the future that, whilst checking the illicit
traffic, would save Government the expense of
keeping up an establishment rendered useless by
the present system. The reply briefly told me that
Government were not at present disposed to make
any change. The necessity for change was however so evident, the folly of flinging away public
money so transparent, I hoped a second attempt
to show it might be more successful.

And now comes a page that might grace the
history of the How not to do it and Circumlocution Offices, so admirably painted by Dickens.
The stolid conservatism of the Council Board was
sufficiently moved to call for a report on my proposals from the Revenue Commissioner, Mr. Vibart,
and, as I afterwards found, from the collectors of
the Guzerat districts. Mr. V—— was not inclined
to take more trouble in the matter than he could
help, and therefore simply replied that as Government had stated that they were not at present
disposed to alter the existing state of things, it

appeared to him unnecessary to offer an opinion on my proposals, and this reply was the only answer I got to my second letter. Most men would think that his opinion being called for, it was his duty to give it, and that the authority so calling for it would have told him so, but he knew Government better.

I was placed in a dilemma. A third application however delicately worded, would seem disrespectful, yet I very much disliked the idea of paying a large sum of money to an encourager of opium-smuggling for work done by me to prevent it. At this time the country was suffering from the effects of drought, and a fund supported by several of the chiefs had been raised for employment of the numerous poor starving creatures that came in search of food to the capital.

So I said to the Jusdhun Wakeel, 'You know that your master patronises smuggling, for he never takes his stipulated quota from the government warehouse, and has had nothing to do with securing the opium now in my hands; on writing to Government about its bestowal they have given an indefinite answer. I don't like to trouble them again, and I don't like to give this money to you ; so if your chief will subscribe a thousand rupees to the famine fund he shall have the rest of his share, otherwise I will refer the matter again, when he may perhaps lose all.' Of course the offer was accepted, and I was enabled to do much good work with the money, useful both to Government and to the people.

Time passed away, and worn with the labour of duties that have since been found to require tenfold the assistance then afforded me, I was sent by the Doctors to the Neilgherries, with injunctions to rest from brain work. Need I mention my surprise whilst there at receiving one day from my successor in Kattywar copy of a correspondence between himself and Government relative to the above transaction, in which I was held to have shown great presumption in unwarrantably fining the Jusdhun chief, to whom the thousand rupees were to be repaid from the public treasury and recovered from me !

All this without any opportunity being afforded

me of offering an explanation. Such are the freaks
of power in a land where there is no public
opinion, or what little there may be, vitiated by
the press being free only to outsiders who know
nothing of the interior workings of the machinery
of Government, and where there is no one empow-
ered to ask awkward questions from the ruling
authority. Here was a case where the public
interest was sacrificed, the public money wasted,
useful reform discountenanced, vicious conduct rewarded, and the officer who attempted first to
prevent and then to remedy the mischief, censured
and punished, because Government had not spared
time to look into a very simple question or to wait
to hear what he might say before passing judgment
on him. The collectors of Guzerat, for whose
opinions my proposals on the opium question
had been sent, reported in their favour, and no one
had even attempted to show any reason against
their adoption.

The error of Government was too glaring to be
persevered in as regards punitive results to myself,
and some flattering language was made use of as

amends for the wrong inflicted, but the treasury suffered, the prestige of provincial authority over the chiefs was lowered, and smuggling left rampant as ever. As I did not return to the Kattywar Agency, I am unaware whether any or what measures were taken to check this, or to keep the chiefs to their agreement.

The connection between the foregoing and the black lion does not at first sight appear, but was in this wise. I have mentioned the havock done in my office by the savage onslaught that saved the lion from mine. The head accountant, though very badly wounded, continued struggling to perform his duties so manfully, and with such hope of recovery, that I made no effort to supply his place. But he died not long after I had left, and when his accounts were made up it appeared that the payments to the Jusdhun chief and to the captors had been entered minus the one thousand rupees transferred to the famine fund, the accounts of which were also kept by the Agency, though not entered in the Government books. Of course the whole sum should have been debited to the parties entitled to receive it, the transfer of the thousand rupees to the charity being a private arrangement. As it was, the audit authorities checked the transaction, and this led to the *dénoûment* I have detailed.

CHAPTER VIII.

FURTHER OBSERVATIONS ON KATTYWAR—PE-
CULIAR USAGE OF BAHAR-WUTTIA — MEANS
ADOPTED BY GOVERNMENT TO DEAL WITH IT,
AND WITH CRIME GENERALLY—CAPTURE OF
CAPTAIN GRANT BY A BAND OF THESE OUT-
LAWS—HIS NARRATIVE OF CAPTIVITY—HINDOO
SUPERSTITIONS.

THE great settlement by Colonel Walker in
1805 left the Peninsula under nearly three
hundred separate jurisdictions, or states, now reduced to less than two hundred. The duty of the
British Agent was to levy their stipulated amount
of tribute in the shares assigned to the Peshwa and
Gaekwar, and to preserve the peace. When the
first failed, the state was placed in charge of
persons who undertook to manage it, and clear off
the debt. Thus, bit by bit, a considerable portion

of the country fell under the more immediate control of the Agency, and for such, as well as for weak states, unable to deal with their own criminals, some system of magisterial and judicial procedure became necessary. A High Criminal Court of Justice was therefore established, with the Political Agent as Chief Judge ; quasi puisne judges called Assessors, being selected for each trial from among the leading men of the country.

This was an excellent measure, for it tended to prevent crime, not only by punishing the offenders, but also by exposing abuses of power that too often gave rise to the offence. In the absence of lawful means of redress, it had long been the custom for aggrieved parties to take the law into their own hands, especially in the case of encroach-ments on land, when the injured owner deemed himself justified in taking to the jungles and hills, enlisting mercenaries, and making war on the state that had wronged him. Scores, nay, hundreds, of cut-throats were always available for a sufficient consideration, and plenty of rival states at hand, where the band were sure of secret support, while fear or favour would generally secure this in his own district. Thus bahar-wuttia had become the established usage. The term literally means *out of country*, a self-imposed outlawry, to be terminated by compromise, capture, or death. These outlaws, as a general rule, only ravaged their own state, but they seldom scrupled to rob, maim, or murder any refusing countenance, or to capture those whose ransom might further their cause.

In 1820 a bahar-wuttia band waylaid and kept captive for nearly three months a British Officer, treating him with a barbarity equalling that shown by King Theodore to the captives it cost us so many millions to release. Notwithstanding the sufferings and hardships endured half a century ago in the most pestilential jungles of the Peninsula during the sickly season of the year, this gentleman, Captain George Grant, still survives as the senior officer of the late Indian Navy, and has, at my request, favoured me with an account of his captivity, of which his modesty has hitherto prevented any published description. Though then only of some ten years' standing, he had brought himself to notice by his daring attacks on the pirates who infested the coast, and had been selected to command the Gaekwar's war vessels employed against them. There was no ascertained connection between the pirates and outlaws, but Captain Grant's office made him a tempting person for the latter to seize, and to hold as a lever to work on the local authorities, and, indeed, they succeeded in their object.

Captain Grant's memoir so well illustrates the anarchy and misrule prevailing in Kattywar, and the peculiar usage which I have described, that I give it entire at the end of this chapter. Bahar-wuttia, I am sorry to say, is not yet thoroughly extirpated, though, happily, not carried on with the savagery of former days. Recent reforms, while greatly diminishing the labours of the British Agency, and increasing its power, have, in fact, tended to give an impetus to the practice, by narrowing, if not closing, the safety-valve formerly open, of appeal to the Agency in cases of violence or fraud, calculated otherwise to drive the subordinate landholder to his old method of obtaining redress. Surely, if we lend our power to the chiefs to put down rebellion, we ought at least to see that they do not force their subjects into it.

When Captain Grant was carried off, the whole Peninsula was more or less controlled by the Gaekwar, whose Viceroy there, was accompanied by an English officer, assistant of the Resident of Baroda. The Viceroy's duty was to levy both his master's and the Peshwa's share of tribute, and to maintain peace. I need scarcely say that the enlargement of the Gaekwar's possessions in the Province was by no means omitted. When the British Government succeeded by conquest to the whole of the Peshwa's dominions, Captain Barnwell was appointed its first Political Agent, shortly after Captain Grant's release. A double rule was speedily done away with, by arrangements with the Baroda Court, and from this period Kattywar has slowly emerged from the condition of which Captain Grant was a victim.

I return from this digression to the Political

Agent's court, certainly not introduced too soon
into the country. The trials held before it brought
to light the usages and superstitions of the people,
and I regret that extreme pressure of official
occupation [1] prevented my preserving notes of
some of the most remarkable. They led to the
suppression of barbarous methods of administering
so-called justice, such as the ordeal of boiling oil,
or of red-hot iron, employed as tests of innocence
or of guilt.

On one occasion I had to try the uncle of the
Palitana Chief, who had gone out into bahar-wuttia
in consequence of the encroachments on his land
by his nephew. I asked the old man why he had
not come to the Agency to complain, instead of
taking the law into his own hands. 'It's not my
fault,' he replied; 'I made the attempt three times,

[1] The duties often devolving on one man in India would scarcely
be credited in this country. In Kattywar they combined every
administrative function over an area of some twenty thousand
square miles, with a population of about two millions.

During the time I held charge, A.D. 1839 to 1843, I had rarely
more than one Assistant, sometimes none. The local Government
has of late become sensible of there being little wisdom in expecting
large results from small means, and has given the Agent half-a-dozen
regular Assistants, besides numerous officers for special duties.

and was always stopped by bad omens. The first time an antelope crossed in front of me the wrong way just after setting out, and, of course, I had to go back; the second attempt I got no omen, till a hare started on my left; the third time, a flight of crows came and perched on a tree on my left, cawing loudly. After such warnings it was folly to try again, so I was obliged to see what I could do for myself, according to the custom of my country.'

Belief in magic is so profound throughout India as to make truth doubly difficult of attainment. In a case of disputed succession that came before me, the symptoms which gave promise of an heir were credited to enchantment, which certain incantations, recited to the sound of a tom-tom in presence of the lady, would infallibly demonstrate; and, on like grounds, a claim to be the lawful heir nearly two years after the death of the husband, has been advanced, and met with support, on the ground that magic, employed by the opposite party, had stayed the birth. There is, indeed, no placing bounds to the credulity of the

Oriental mind not trained in habits of thought, and simple conversion to Christianity, without such training, makes little, if any, difference. I have been petitioned by a Christian woman, in virtue of my magisterial authority, to compel another to undo a spell cast on her. The miracles of the Gospel are as nothing to a Hindoo. One of their holy men drank up the ocean—what then need be said of the feats of their gods! Miracles are everywhere believed to be worked at the present day. The whole land appears to its inhabitants to be peopled by spirits of diverse orders. The village deities, when required, predict events in various ways; a common method is to attach a grain of rice to the eyebrows or breasts of the idol, if the right one adheres longest the omen is propitious, and *vice versâ*; or some devotee works himself into a frenzy before the shrine, in which condition his utterances are held to be those of the god. To recount all the superstitions prevalent would fill a volume. Though varying in different provinces, a general family likeness runs through all of Hindoo descent; many of these also prevail

among the Mòhammedans, how far originally im-
ported and how far borrowed it would be difficult
to say.

NARRATIVE OF CAPTIVITY OF CAPTAIN GEORGE GRANT, LATE INDIAN NAVY.

'In 1813 I' was appointed by the Bombay
Government, at the request of Captain Carnac,
Resident of Baroda, to the command of the naval
force then established by His Highness the Gaekwar for the suppression of the Indian and Arabian
pirates that infested the coasts of Kattywar and
Kutch. We captured and destroyed several, and
in 1820 they were so much reduced that the Gaekwar abolished his naval establishment, not considering it necessary to keep it up any longer. I
then received orders to proceed inland from my
station at Velun Bunder, or Diu Head, to
Amrelle, to deliver over charge of my vessels to
the Gaekwar's Sersooba, or Dewan, in Kattywar.
On my way I was attacked by a bhar-wuttee, or

outlaw Kattee, named Bawawalla, with thirty-five horsemen. My horsekeeper was killed, my moonshee severely wounded, and two of my escort of four horsemen also wounded. I could not myself make any resistance, having only a riding whip.

'On first coming up Bawawalla said that he wanted to consult me about his affairs, and on this pretext got me to dismount. My people being rendered helpless, I was forced to remount my horse and gallop off with the gang, who took me into a large jungle, called the Geer, where I was kept prisoner on the top of a mountain for two months and seventeen days. During the whole of this time two armed men with swords drawn kept guard over me. I laid amongst the rocks drenched with rain night and day, with the exception of two nights, when the gang forced me to accompany them, and we stopped in a friendly village. In this expedition I was occasionally allowed to ride, but always surrounded by a strong band that made all attempt to escape impossible. In one village where the people favoured Bawawalla the women took my part, and upbraided him and his men for my cruel

treatment. Towards unfriendly villages the custom
of the gang was to ride up to the gates and chop
off the heads of little boys at play, and then go off
rejoicing and laughing at their cursed exploits.
When they returned to the encampment after a
day's murdering foray, the young Kattees used to
boast how many men they had killed, and one day
I heard the old fellows questioning them rather
particularly whether or not they were sure they
had killed their victims. "Yes," they said; they
had seen their spears through them, and were
certain they were dead. "Ah," remarked an old
Kattee, "a human being is worse to kill than any
other animal; never be sure they are dead till
you see the body on one side of the road, and
the head on the other."

'At times the chief, Bawawalla, in a state of
stupor from opium, would come and sit by my
side, and holding his dagger over me, ask how
many stabs it would take to kill me. I said I
thought one would do, and I hoped he would put
me out of misery. "I suppose you think," he
would answer, "that I won't kill you; I have killed

as many human beings as ever fisherman killed
fish, and I should think nothing of putting an end
to you; but I shall keep you a while yet, till I see
if your Government will get me back my property,
if so I will let you off."

'When not out plundering the gang slept most
of the day. At night the halter of each horse was
tied to its master's arm; when the animals heard
voices they tugged, and the men were up in an
instant. Their meals consisted of Bajree cakes
with chillies and milk when it could be got. I
used to have the same. Once or twice my servant
was allowed to come to me, and brought the rare
treat of some curry and a bottle of claret from
Captain Ballantine. The wine Bawawalla seized
on at once, thinking it was daroo or spirits, but on
tasting the liquor he changed his mind, and spitting
it out declared it was poison sent no doubt on purpose
to kill him. By way of test I was ordered to drink
it, which I did with very great pleasure, and finding
me none the worse he gave up his idea of poison.

'Among his people there were two young men
who showed some feeling for me. One of these

was shot in a pillaging raid shortly before my release. They used to try and cheer me up by telling me I should be set free. Occasionally, when opportunity offered, they would inform me how many people they had killed, and the method they pursued when rich travellers refused to pay the sum demanded. This was to tie the poor wretches by their legs to a beam across a well, with their heads touching the water, and then to saw away at the rope until the tortured victims agreed to their demands, then the Kattees would haul them up, get from them a *hoondee*, or bill, on some agent, and keep them prisoners till this was paid.

'Sometimes they told me of their master's intention to murder me, which was not pleasant. He and his men had many disputes about me just as his hopes or fears of the consequence of my imprisonment prevailed.

'I can never forget one stormy night, they were all sitting round a great fire—I lay behind them. Lions and wild beasts roared around us, but did not prevent me overhearing a debate upon the subject of what should be done with me. The men complained that they had been two months in the jungle on my account, their families were in the villages very badly off for food, and that they would stay no longer. Their chief replied, "Let us kill him, and flee to some other part of the country." To this they objected that the English would send troops and take their families prisoners and ill-use them. So in the end it was agreed to keep me for the present.

'My release was effected at last through our Political Agent, Captain Ballantine, who prevailed on the Nawab of Joonaghur to use his influence to get another Kattee who had forcibly taken Bawa-walla's *Pergunna*, or district, to restore it to him, and Bawawalla thus having gained his object, set me free.

'My sufferings during confinement were almost beyond endurance, and I used to pray in the evening that I might never see another morning. I had my boots on my feet for the first month, not being able to get them off from the constant wet until I was reduced by sickness. Severe fever,

I

with ague and inflammation of liver, came on, and with exposure to the open air drove me delirious, so that when let go I was found wandering in the fields at night covered with vermin from head to foot. I shall never forget the heavenly sensation of the hot bath and clean clothes I got in the tent of the Nawab of Joonaghur's Dewan, the officer who accomplished my release. The fever and ague then contracted continued on me for five years, and the ill effects still remain, my head being at times greatly troubled with giddiness, and I have severe fits of ague; my memory also is much affected, but I can never forget the foregoing incidents, though it is now upwards of fifty years since they occurred.

'G. GRANT.

'BARHOLM HOUSE, CREETOWN, N.B. :
'*April*, 1871.'

Extract from the ' *Bombay Courier,*' *April* 24, 1824.

'By intelligence from Kattywar, we learn that the notorious Bawawalla has at last met with the fate he has so long merited. He was attacked on the 6th inst. in Bessawudder by Hursoor, a Katty chief with whom he had long been at enmity, and was slain by him in a desperate conflict.

'It may be in the recollection of many of our readers that this person in 1820 carried off Lieutenant Grant of the H. C. Marine, while in the Gaekwar's service, and kept him in captivity for three months, during which time he was treated with the most savage cruelty. For some years past Bawawalla has been little heard of, but having lately resumed his former predatory course, apprehensions were entertained that he would be the cause of disturbances in that part of the country, when his career has been thus unexpectedly closed by death.'[1]

[1] In this and the previous Chapter allusion has been made to the opium-consuming habits of the people. The amount they can take without seemingly shortening life appears almost incredible. A bhar-wuttia leader, by name Champrajwala, another Bawawala, though less ferocious, had, in conflict with some of our troops, shot an officer of the 15th Native Infantry. He was at last secured and made over to the Political Agent for trial. Whilst in gaol, the Civil-Surgeon informed me so ill had the prisoner become from deprivation of opium that to keep him alive he was obliged daily to increase his dose to the astounding quantity of seventy grains, that on reducing this more than a few grains he again fell ill, and that he could never reach a moderate minimum without being again obliged

to increase the allowance. Champrajwala was convicted and sentenced to imprisonment for life, and transferred some four-and-thirty years ago to the Ahmedabad gaol, whence, many years after, he made a bold attempt to escape. He was ultimately liberated, and, for aught I know, may be still alive—his habitual dose of opium was the size of a large pigeon's egg.

CHAPTER IX.

HINDOO SUPERSTITIONS CONTINUED—OUR LAWS
NOT ADAPTED TO THE CHARACTER OF THE
PEOPLE.

EARLY in 1844 I was placed in charge of the
Sawunt Waree territory during an insurrection that had broken out there in concert with
another simultaneously raging above the Ghats in
the Southern Mahratta country. I found the State
unable to meet current expenses, and the reform
of its finances had in consequence to be effected.
Among numerous items of expenditure struck off
or reduced was a monthly payment to a demon
called King of the Hobgoblins. His Majesty's
palace was the forest, and he was propitiated every
night by a meal placed outside the gateway of the
fort which held the Raja's palace, and also, amongst
other buildings, the dwelling of the Political Superintendent.

The Minister of the State, a worthy old man, and devout Brahmin, was not answerable for the wild doings of others, and I used to invite him with a few more to sit with me on the magisterial bench, consulting them from time to time, and attending to their opinions at discretion. These all expressed more or less alarm on learning my intention to withhold the demon's grant. It might draw his vengeance down on the fort, they said. I silenced, if not convinced them, by asking them to reflect whether the Company's government had not proved itself stronger than all the demons of the land put together. That I, as representative of the British power, now faced the gateway, and it was insulting to me to suppose that I could not take better care of the fort than the hobgoblins, all of whom I defied, and in whose existence I disbelieved. 'Depend upon it,' I continued, 'if mischief follow, I will trace the human agent, and make him answer for it.'

As the circumstances of the time had called forth striking exhibitions of corrective power, no one liked to bell the cat, so the mice remained in their

holes, and the spirit world of Sawunt Waree acknowledged British supremacy.

Advantage may at times be taken of the superstitions of the people for their benefit. I was one
day riding across country in Kattywar, when I
observed a man continually throwing stones to his
right and left as he followed the pathway. I
fancied him a maniac, but rode up, and enquired
what he was doing? ' An act of religion ' (dhurm),
he replied. ' How so?' I asked. ' Don't you see,'
he answered, 'how these sharp stones gall the
bullocks, and injure their hoofs as they tread the
path with their loads? I am on a pilgrimage to
Dwarka, and before setting out made a vow to
clear off these stones the whole of the way.'

Macadamised roads were then unknown save at
our own stations. Those throughout the provinces
were what nature and the wear and tear of transit
made them.

Many years afterwards, when Political Agent in
Kutch, I was anxious to obtain a more direct road
from the capital to its chief seaport than the one
then existing, which was nothing better than a

beaten track over a steep and difficult Ghat.[1] The Rao being a conservative of the *stare super anti-quas vias* type, was hard to move towards any new thing. I expatiated on the saving of some miles in distance, and therefore of time, labour, and cost of transport, &c., but all in vain, until I bethought me of telling him the anecdote above related. 'Scores of bullocks are annually destroyed and lamed on the present Ghat road,' I wound up with, 'will your Highness allow yourself to be outdone by that poor pilgrim?' The argument was conclusive, the road was ordered, money for it set apart, and it was opened, though not completed, when I left in the close of 1856, Captain Raikes and Captain Shortt rendering effective aid throughout.

Another road-making anecdote will illustrate native feeling unchanged by contact with European civilisation. Sawunt Waree having proved a hotbed of disturbance, Mr. Richard Spooner was in 1838 appointed to control it. One of the first things he wisely did was to make a good road to

---

[1] Hill or mountain pass.

connect its capital with the seaport Vingorla. At this time Major Troward was charged with the duty of forming a disciplined body out of the armed retainers of the state, and was on friendly terms with the Raja, whose power had been superseded. One day, in confidential mood, the latter remarked to him, ' See how this Sahib is spoiling my country by his new road, and what he calls improvements!' I ought perhaps to add, as some excuse for the Raja, that the traditionary policy of the state was to maintain inaccessibility. Forests, difficult passes, vile roads, thick jungles, were the bulwarks not only of the capital, but of most of its towns and villages.

With such ignorance prevailing, the path of justice is indeed beset with thorns, and the people easily swindled and deluded. For instance, soon after I had assumed charge of this State, an impostor went about the country levying a war cess in my name ; his credentials an empty gooseberry bottle of Crosse and Blackwell, the Royal arms in gilt letters on its label, and a paper of sham English writing, headed by a supposed official seal that was merely the impression made by the bung of a mustard jar. Yet these precious credentials had sufficed for several villages, till he was unwise enough to venture where he met with a functionary sufficiently acute to deal with him. When on his trial, all the foregoing was fully proved. The liability of the people to be defrauded by the subordinates of Government is a cogent reason against the imposition of new taxes. Our imperfect and tedious system of redress, often aggravating rather than compensating wrong, renders it imperative on Government, as much as possible, to abstain from such, however sound in theory. And this leads me to speak of the working of our courts, little understood by Englishmen, who imagine law a panacea for every evil.

Our system is unsuited to the Oriental mind, except where imbued with Western ideas, as in the Presidency towns, though even here it is no safeguard for the poorer classes. Throughout the interior the masses dread our courts and their processes, and many a wrong is endured rather than seek redress through them. We have, alas! to

answer for much cruelty in forcing reluctant plain-
tiffs and witnesses to travel immense distances,
detaining them weeks or months from their homes,
in order that white men who had injured them
might be tried before the Presidency Courts, where
the interim death of a witness or the browbeating
of timid ones, a law quibble or a *nigger*-hating
juryman, too often rendered the whole process vain.
Up to the time of my leaving India this was the
privilege of our roughs in the interior, and attempts
to remedy so iniquitous a state of the law were
always frustrated by national and legal prejudices.

Of late the amalgamation of the Supreme and
Sudder Courts, with their judges visiting the interior on circuit, has done a good deal to mitigate the
crying injustice. But the system of punishing
witnesses is not limited to trials of Europeans. A
thief had stolen from a native in Bombay some
copper cooking-pots, and escaped with them to the
Sawunt Waree territory, from which I traced him
to that of Goa, before he had time to dispose of his
plunder. The Portuguese Government, with their
usual friendliness, made him over with his stolen

goods to my border functionary, whence he and they were passed on to me. Now, the Bombay authorities required the attendance, as witnesses, of all who had been instrumental in securing the thief and the stolen property at the several stations where the latter had changed hands, so that, in addition to the prisoner, I was obliged to send half-a-dozen of them to Bombay. They had never before left their own country. Some were Brahmins, to whom a sea voyage was a horror, for no Brahmin may eat anything cooked at sea,[1] and at that season the native craft, miserable comfortless things, which alone carried on the coast trade, took ten days or a fortnight for the voyage. The land journey was out of the question. The poor fellows were in despair, and some in employ of the state offered to resign rather than go, but there was no help for it, and they were sent off. Eleven days of sickness and starvation were passed on board, and shortly after reaching Bombay, where they had to shelter themselves as best they could in a land of strangers, they were informed that the trial had been

[1] Several other Hindoo castes suffer in the same way.

put off to the next sessions. So they had to remain, and wrote piteous appeals to me for relief. After three months of great inconvenience to them and to the interests of the little State, from which two of them could ill be spared, they were directed to attend the Supreme Court, there to await the dreaded badgering of witnesses that our law to its discredit allows. They came, and after waiting some hours, had the satisfaction of seeing the prisoner walk past them with a jeering salaam, and of learning that the judge had directed his acquittal as no prosecutor had appeared. After this, permission was given them to return home, and I fear they brought back no very exalted ideas of British justice.

Another story will also show the inapplicability of our system to men of the interior, if not to natives generally. I had in my employ a painter named Jooma, to draw for me figures and costumes of the people of Kutch,—a respectable, inoffensive man, and a stranger to the world beyond it. I tempted him, however, to accompany me in December 1856 to Bombay, there to finish some work he had on hand. We landed on the 19th, and Jooma obtained a temporary lodging in the town. Three or four days after this, he brought me a paper, saying a peon had given it him with directions to attend the magistrate's court, asking me what the paper was, and what he should do. It proved to be a summons to appear and answer for the infraction of some municipal law on the 9th of the month. I told him that he must of course attend, and say that he was at that time some five hundred miles away, and that he had only just arrived with me in Bombay, of all which I gave him a formal certificate. On the day named he attended the court, where he was hustled into a box with several others, guarded by peons, who would not let him speak, till, with great difficulty, he managed to get my certificate handed up to the magistrate. This gentleman informed him that he could pay no attention to communications so received. After some further, to poor Jooma equally unintelligible, processes, each prisoner was ordered to be fined ten rupees, and to be kept in custody till paid.

It is needless to say, that I did not remain quiet under this perversion of justice. It appeared, on enquiry, that the magistrate, perhaps not well up in the native languages, could prove by witnesses that all the accused, Jooma included, had pleaded guilty, and consequently had not considered it necessary to go into the evidence. An action, therefore, against him would fail; but the fine was given back, and Jooma returned to his own land a wiser man than he left it, with less of punishment in his lessons than many an innocent but friendless prisoner has had to endure from the misfortune of getting entangled in any of our Law Courts. I relate this incident as an example of the mischief perpetually done by a system of procedure unsuited to the native character. If Government wish to mitigate its severity and injustice towards the masses, they will assign to all the courts a competent person, whose duty it should be to guard the ignorant from being entrapped in its meshes—a sort of poor man's counsel, in short, but liable to removal on due cause assigned by the presiding judge or magistrate.

A case came before me at Sawunt Waree, in which the gravamen of the plaintiff was the defendant having wished Goa justice to fall upon his house, besides other abusive speech. At a loss for the meaning, I asked the good old minister, Lely Punt, sitting by me, to explain it, which he did in this wise: 'You probably know that all our southern districts have fallen into possession of the Portuguese, on which the population had to settle their quarrels or seek redress for their wrongs at Goa. But the law's delays there were interminable, generally ending in the ruin of both parties, so that a Goa lawsuit has become proverbial in this country for a curse, and the wish for anybody to become involved in one considered highly injurious language.'

I am not aware of any great superiority in our legal systems over those of our European brethren of Portuguese India, and it would be well if our legislators will take the hint. What is wanted for the masses is simplicity of means and speedy decisions. The way in which in our courts the interests and feelings of witnesses are sacrificed to the real or supposed benefit of prisoners, or to legal formalities, is a cause of general complaint. And the difficulties of bringing crime home to those committing it, are increased to a dangerous extent, all of which, acts as a hotbed for its growth.

The States bordering on our own specially suffer : although they may be administered by British offiters, and have courts of judicature under the supervision of our Government, unless a thief from our parts be caught *flagrante delictu*, he has to be prosecuted before his own courts, perhaps days' journey away, instead of before that of the district in which he committed the crime. Such is the one-sided character of our rule. An intelligent native minister of one of the border states of Kattywar once remarked to me, ' Sir, you profess to do justice, but you encourage crime and punish the innocent whilst letting off the guilty. Lying is now found the best way of escaping the consequences of evil doing. With us it was always considered the worst.' The facts he stated showed that he had too much reason for his belief.

During the insurrection in Sawunt Waree of

K

1844-45, persons having quarrels with their neigh-
bours took advantage of the general confusion to
induce or even hire stray bodies of insurgents to
murder their enemies.   Through the friendly conduct of the Portuguese Government more than fifty
of these cut-throats, tracked to Goa villages, were
from time to time, given up to me for trial.   In
former days Sawunt Waree having been addicted
to piracy our Government had taken from it a
narrow strip all along the sea coast, thus shutting it
out from such occupation.   The boundary line ran
north and south pretty much as if done by compass,
in this way cutting through a village now known as
Asolee and Arolee.   Here the luckless inhabitants
often fell under double jurisdictions.

On one occasion, a gang of some thirty men,
led by villagers who bore enmity to a leading
person therein, attacked the place in broad daylight,
and murdered him, his brother and a son, spite of
the courageous attempts of the wife and mother to
defend them.   Some of the death-strokes were
dealt on one side of the border, some on the other.
I could only deal with those on mine.   One by

one the criminals were traced and captured, some liable to my jurisdiction, others to that of Rutnagerry near a hundred miles away, but to which I was forced to consign them. During the course of two years, repeated trials took place, there, and at Sawunt Waree, at which the widow who had known and recognised the assassins, was of course an essential witness. She was a remarkably handsome woman of about forty-five, with a commanding cast of countenance and clear metallic voice. I shall never forget what happily proved the last trial, at least in my court, of her patience. On stepping into the witness-box she threw her saree around her and drew herself up like a Roman matron. Her eyes seemed to flash fire as she cried —'Hear what I have to say. How often do you wish to tear my wounds open. These men only committed murder once, but you and the Company's people are more cruel. You keep killing me afresh. Since that dreadful day I have had no peace. I am sent for here, there, and everywhere, to you, to Vingorla, to Malwan, to Rutnaggery. My sandals are worn out with walking all these distances, and my heart perpetually torn. I know no rest, always looking for a fresh summons so long as one of the band survives. Would that they had killed me as well as my husband. Have I not stated the same thing over and over again? Have you not got it all written down? Have I told lies that you keep continually asking me the same questions? Why do you persecute me so?'

Poor woman, I pitied her from my heart, but I was helpless.

I have shown how our legal system harasses the innocent, and will now give an instance how it spares the guilty. Of all the petty chiefs in the insurrection of 1844–45, none were more cruel or so mischievous as Baba Bhogta, who got together some half-hundred odd men of his own stamp, and laid himself out to do the general murdering business of the country: keeping his band ready on hire for the gratification of private grudges. This man escaped over the border with other insurgent leaders pressed by Colonel Outram's field detachments, and surrendered with them to the Portuguese. The Goa Government disarmed

and confined them, but otherwise treated them as
political refugees. When, however, I could show
felonies committed unconnected with the rebellion,
individuals were from time to time surrendered.
Amongst such was Baba Bhogta. Unfortunately,
there was paucity of *judicial* proof for the murders
done on my side the border, but clear evidence of
some within the 'Company's' frontier, wherefore I
made him over to the magistrate with an explana-
tory statement. Some time afterwards, the police
officer I had placed in his village reported that
Baba Bhogta had been seen entering his house, in
which the mother continued to reside. The filial
attachment of even cruel felons to their parents is
a redeeming trait in their character. They will run
great risks rather than not say farewell if doomed
to separation. One of my own prisoners under
sentence of death, had escaped from the Waree
jail and fort by combined ingenuity, dexterity, and
daring, and had, though heavily ironed, traversed
the jungles for a dozen miles to his mother's cot-
tage. I of course concluded that Baba Bhogta had
escaped from the Rutnagerry jail, as he had before

nearly done at Goa, wherefore that same night his house was surrounded, and next morning he was brought in to me a prisoner. I could not well believe his story that the great folk in Bombay had found him innocent, and ordered his release, whereupon he had returned to his village like any other peaceful citizen. A part, however, proved true; he had been condemned to death by the Judicial Commissioner on clear proof of several brutal murders, but a flaw had been found in these having been made instances of treason, and he was a subject of the Sawunt Waree State. So one of the most dangerous men in the country was let loose on society in due routine fashion without so much as any notice given to me, for what has law to do with politics?

To turn from the tragic to somewhat of the comic. A curious case of treasure trove came before me. A woman out working in a field found a ring of some size standing up from the ground in a place where water, having worn away the earth, had left it exposed. On trying to lift it, up she found it fixed and immovable. Superstitious fears led her to abstain from any further attempt until she could consult the village temple. This done she was informed by the hierophant that it would be exceedingly dangerous to have anything to do with the ring till the spirit of the place had been propitiated, and that she might thank her star that she had not been struck dead in her attempt to pull it up. But he would perform all the proper ceremonies that very night, obtain an omen to guide future action, and let her know on the morrow the result. So, fully satisfied and nothing doubting, the woman went home.

That night the priest sallied out with two companions armed with proper implements for obtaining the omen. After some tough digging, they unearthed several engraved copper-plates fastened by the ring. Beneath these a pot, no doubt containing coin. This being removed, they put back the plates, covering them with earth, and leaving all as much as possible as before. The next thing was to carry the pot to the village temple, and lay it before the shrine, when the priest promised due apportionment of the contents, after permission of the god had been obtained, and it could safely be done.

Next morning the woman was told that the priest had secured her from the molestation of evil spirits, and that she might now ascertain the nature of the ring. This was accordingly done, and the copper-plates before mentioned obtained. They were covered with ancient characters, and corroded, evidently very old, and the diggers thought it rather odd that they should come up so easily.

Meanwhile, the man who had actually carried the pot the previous night, being of inferior position to the other two, on going to claim his share of the contents from the priest, found that he had left the village, as also had his colleague. It was evident to the fellow that he had been sold in this affair, so out of revenge he at once gave information to the local police officer, who lost no time in sending word to me, and in pursuing the runaways. The village was, however, within a day's journey of the border, where my authority ceased, and that of the Kumpanee Bahadoor began, under which very free scope is allowed for fraud. On inspecting the plates, I found them engraved in the Sanskrit of a remote period. They referred to grants made during the reign of the Chalookya dynasty over this quarter of India, from twelve to fifteen centuries ago. And if my reader have antiquarian tendencies, he may judge with what eagerness I longed to recover the coins of that period, that the pot buried with the plates doubtless contained. It is only by such waifs and strays that we can hope to fill up, in some slight degree, the interstices of Hindoo history, now so obscure and uncertain. I authorised double payment, in current coin, of the value of any so found, but in vain.

On the return of the absentees to their village, they were sent in to me for trial. All I have mentioned was fully proved, and the two offenders were sentenced to imprisonment. I think they must have disposed of the coins beyond recovery, or my offer to pay them so much more than they were worth, and to mitigate their punishment, would have brought them to light. The fraud of the village priest was, however, established, to the improvement of the future morals of his community, and the Bombay Branch of the Royal Asiatic Society got the benefit of the historic plates.

The climax of superstition is reached in the Hindoo rite of Suttee, and great was the number of its victims in Kutch. Few villages there of any size failed to give testimony to the heroism of their widows in the monuments called Pallias, resembling our tombstones, that line the entrance road, distinguished by the sign of a bloody hand, engraved and painted on them. Other Pallias commemorated the death of all who fell in defence of their village, or in any war by sea or land. Rude figures of a ship in the one case, or of a warrior on horseback in the other, denoted which, while the name of the deceased, with the date and nature of the occurrence, was also shown in the stone.

The rite of Suttee was held to be the highest exhibition of religious virtue, and the victim venerated as a saint, from whose hands a grain of the rice scattered before immolation, became a treasured charm. Such being the state of public feeling, the Rao had been deaf to the advice of the several

Agents of Government at his court; and, as we were bound by treaty not to interfere with his administration beyond certain stipulated limits, and to respect the religious practices of the people, the custom still prevailed at the time of which I speak.

One day, in 1852, when His Highness was in the north of his dominions, my Assistant in the east, and myself in the west, Dr. Bloxham, the Civil Surgeon, who as such became a temporary Assistant at head-quarters for routine work, received tidings that a Suttee was coming off near the town. He had had no experience of the duties of his office, and supposing it incumbent on him to stop at all hazards so barbarous a deed, mounted his horse, and rode down to the place of sacrifice, which he reached just as the pile was lighted. Jumping off his horse, he rushed forward, and almost by main force dragged the widow from the dead body of her husband, well nigh through the flames.

It was well for him that our power had been so thoroughly established over the minds of the people, and in any case, that some fanatic, carried away by this outrage on the religious feelings of the mourners, did not cut him down. As it was, murmurs of disapproval arose on all sides, while the would-be victim uttered the most passionate imprecations and protests, vowing that such tyranny had never before been done under English rule, and that if she was not allowed to burn she would die otherwise, but never leave the spot. The worthy doctor confessed to me afterwards that he had never been so cursed in his life, and trusted not to be so again.

At last, with difficulty, the woman was persuaded to take shelter in a neighbouring temple, and there her disowned champion left her, to go home himself, and write particulars to me.

I could not approve of his doings, though dictated by the purest philanthropy. But I urged the Rao to seize this opportunity of stopping the barbarous rite altogether; the more so as the onus of doing it in the present instance had not fallen on him. He returned at once to his capital, and in company with Dr. Bloxham proceeded to the

temple where the widow remained, and urged her
to desist from her intention, promising her any
support or assistance she might require. 'What!'
she replied to him, 'do you, my Prince, take part
against me with these unbelieving and cruel
Sahibs! I am ashamed of you. But it is no use.
You may hinder me from burning, but you can't
make me eat and drink. Die, one way or another,
I will. Why should you seek to separate me from
my husband?'

This heroine of a dark creed was of middle age,
and of the middle class of life. Nothing in her
worldly condition tempted her to suicide. Some
of the small bones from the ashes of the funeral-
pile were collected for her, and, with these, in a
small bag tied as a necklace, she remained in the
temple night and day, refusing all nourishment,
until the Rao felt he could no longer resist her
claim, and gave permission for another pile. She
went to it triumphantly, and perished, calm and
resolute to the end.

Such was the last authorised Suttee in Kutch.[1]

[1] Lord Dalhousie overlooked this fact in his *précis*, drawn up on
leaving India. This is not a singular instance of his inattention to

Although my pictures are confined to experiences of the political officer, I am tempted to add a pendant from an earlier period of like resolution and devotion in the opposite sex.

When with my regiment I used occasionally to visit the hospital to see how the men of my company were. In 1827 Surgeon Conwell was our medical officer, a somewhat rough Irishman, whose patients were certainly not likely to be malingerers. He had great contempt for caste, and 'all that Hindoo nonsense.' One day he addressed me: 'Oh, Jacob, I'm glad you've come! Here's a fellow of yours dying merely because he's a fool, and won't drink brandy. Speak to him; he'll listen to you perhaps. Tell him he has nothing whatever the matter with him but exhaustion from the fever that has left him, and if I can keep up his strength

the affairs of the 'Minor Presidencies.' As Kutch has an area of between four and five thousand square miles, and up to the conquest of Sind was our most important frontier province on the west, it could not legitimately be treated on the *de minimus*, &c. maxim. In like manner he enlarged on the measures taken for the suppression of Infanticide in the countries more directly under his rule, whilst the more continued and more successful efforts of the Western Presidency are unnoticed.

for a day or two, nature will have time to rally, and he'll be as well as ever ; else death is certain.' The patient was a good soldier, and one of the best shots in my company. I found him quite sensible and glad to see me, but nothing could shake his resolution. ' The Doctor wants me to drink brandy,' he said ; ' 'tis against my caste, and I won't do it.' Had stimulants been given disguised under some other name than spirits, the man might not have objected, but the Doctor could not stoop to folly such as this. On my earnest warning that death was inevitable unless he took the medicine, the Sepoy replied, ' Sahib, I prefer to die rather than live polluted,' and so he passed away.

CHAPTER X.

THE PERSIAN WAR—THE FIRST OUTBREAK OF MUTINY IN WESTERN INDIA.

IN December, 1856, I left Kutch for Bombay, with the intention of retiring from a service in which proofs of distinction by the local Government became, under the Procustes' bed application of Horse Guard ideas, disqualification for promotion. Under this system such men as Munro, Malcolm, Outram, Lawrence, and numbers like them, were singled out for supersession, unless they had done three years' regimental duty as lieutenant-colonels, or might have been fortunate enough to escape this lot by a previous brevet. To render the thing more absurd, exceptions were made in favour of men who did no military duty whatever worthy of the name, such as making roads or barracks, or issuing stores; while a political officer, take Herbert Edwardes for instance, had he been then a lieutenant-colonel, instead of a simple lieutenant, commanding thousands of irregular troops and fighting pitched battles, in short, performing the highest duties of a general officer, would have been liable to supersession.

Among the Bombay officers I stood next in the line of lieutenant-colonels to Sir James Outram, happily saved, together with my junior Sir Henry Lawrence, from my fate by previous brevet, and I was too high up in the general list to make any regimental service effectual to accelerate promotion. Sir James, on returning from England to command the Persian expedition, found me out in Bombay, and tempted me to accompany him by the offer of a command. The history of this successful campaign has yet to be written. Although very similar to the Abyssinian affair, as regards numbers and the necessity of having its base of operations in Bombay, so that the very hay for our horses was sent from thence, it had no attraction for English eyes or newspapers; no special correspondent enlivened the public with

L

pictures coloured as they only can be on the spot
and at the time, albeit there was much to interest.
By the way, it was lucky for many a good soldier
we had to carry the said hay, for being compressed
in large bales nearly as hard as bricks it was in-
geniously employed as a rampart to all the trans-
ports on the side next the enemy as we steamed
up the Euphrates exposed to artillery and infantry
fire, whereby but few casualties occurred amongst
the men, though possibly some broken teeth
among the horses. I am afraid to say how many
bullets one bale alone was found to contain.

Peace concluded, the force broke up, and the
major part returned to Bombay in May 1857,
where our first greeting was the news of the terrible rising in the East, and the re-establishment of
the Great Mogul on his throne. Lord Elphinstone,
then Governor of Bombay, whose self-possession,
unselfishness and vigilance, from first to last, cannot be too highly praised, sent off the European
portion of our force to the assistance of our brethren in Bengal, for all seemed quiet in the West.
But great uneasiness pervaded the public mind;

and from my intimate acquaintance with the native character and state of general feeling, I feared that similar causes might produce similar effects as well in one part of India as in the other; for though our native army was exempt from some of the evils under which that of Bengal suffered, yet too much had been done in the attempt to Anglo-Saxonise the Sepoy; too little attention paid to the idiosyncrasies of the race, and the control of their commanders too greatly weakened to give us any real security, and I wrote in to Government my reasons for fearing the spread of the contagion. As events proved, the quiet was but a calm before the storm which shortly afterwards burst upon us.

During the night of July 31, the very middle of the monsoon, the 27th Native Infantry, stationed at Kolapoor, rose in arms, and detailed parties to attack their officers' bungalows. The native adjutant, a Jew, and a Hindoo Havildar (Serjeant), ran to give warning barely in time to permit the ladies to fly from their houses before the Sepoys came up, and poured volleys into them. Captain

M'Culloch and a few others endeavoured to rally some of the corps around them, but only sham assistance was given, and they were fortunate in escaping with their lives. The Government treasure-chest and bazaar were plundered, and riot reigned supreme. Three officers who had escaped into the country were shot and thrown into the river; the rest took refuge in the Residency, about a mile from Camp, but near the lines of the Kolapoor Local Infantry. This corps was commanded by an excellent officer, beloved and respected by his men, Captain John Schneider, now Colonel and Judge Advocate General of the Bombay Army.

Government alone by telegraph was acquainted with this outbreak. But such had been the whisperings in the bazaars, and the rumours of sedition from many quarters, that the European community in Bombay had taken alarm, and numbers conveyed their wives and children to the shipping in the harbour. The civilians furnished volunteer horse that patrolled the streets at night; meetings were held to discuss points of rendezvous and best modes of defence ; everyone burnished up his weapons, and there was a general feeling of distrust, not lessened by the fact that, through the exertions of Mr. Forjett, the excellent and energetic Superintendent of Police, some of the sepoys in garrison were found to be untrustworthy.

Such was the state of affairs when, unconscious of the reason, I received orders from the Commander-in-chief, Sir Henry Somerset, to wait upon him at Poona ; though still, nominally, Political Agent in Kutch, the order placing me at His Excellency's disposal for the Persian campaign had not been cancelled. Whilst preparing to start, another letter reached me, this time from the Governor, commanding my attendance at Parell; where, on arrival, Lord Elphinstone informed me of what had occurred at Kolapoor, and that I had been sent for by the Chief to receive the command of the troops in that quarter, but that there were none to be depended on, except perhaps the local regiments, which were under civil authority; he desired to unite all under one head, and otherwise give me special political authority to meet the exigencies of the situation ;

but before making up his mind what to do, as he was very unwilling to supersede Colonel Maughan, then Political Superintendent of Kolapoor, His Excellency desired me to wait until he could receive further information. I replied, that I must immediately proceed to Poona, in obedience to the orders of the Chief, who might be offended at any delay on my part. The Governor answered, that he would make matters right by explaining to Sir Henry Somerset that he had kept me, and he then and there telegraphed accordingly from his own room. But no particulars arrived the next day (Colonel Maughan, as it transpired afterwards, distrusting the telegraph office), and the Governor delayed no longer to commission me for the work. My orders were brief and satisfactory. 'I am aware,' said Lord Elphinstone, 'that in a crisis like this a person on the spot ought to be the best judge of any action that might be at once necessary; to wait for orders may allow events to become too strong to master. I have confidence in your judgment; do your best to meet the present emergency, and rely on my full support.'

The poets of old would have said the gods had descended to delay my progress to Poona, for I met with nothing but misadventures throughout the journey. First, my carriage broke down *en route* to the railway station, and I thereby lost the night train. The rail was then completed only to the foot of the Ghats, and trains ran but twice a day. The next morning I reached the Ghats, and there all manner of impediments occurred in getting up. On arriving at the top, not a horse or vehicle was to be procured till the afternoon, when I once more made a start, only to be brought up in the middle of a dark rainy night by one of the horses falling and lying as dead for a considerable time, the carriage half overturned, so that I reached Poona the day after I was expected, and found the Adjutant-General gone, and the Chief impatiently awaiting my arrival.

I rather thought that the Governor had not entirely made things smooth for me; but be that as it may, the Chief gave me every authority in his power to confer, said that a troop of horse artillery and of dragoons waited for me at Satara to be my

escort to Kolapoor, and cautioned me against proceeding without sufficient guard, lest a similar fate
should befall me to that of Colonel Ovans,[1] and
finally ordered me to report direct to head-quarters.
It was clear that Sir Henry Somerset had no
intention of being caught napping, for I found
quite a detachment of European soldiers at his doorway, and everything in Poona betokened extreme
vigilance and caution. Through the delay caused
by the accidents of my journey, I was just too late
to take advantage for further progress of horses
laid on the Satara road to bring off the Rajas.[2]
While waiting for a fresh relay I received from Mr.
Bettington, Commissioner of Police, proofs of correspondence between the Arch-Moolvee conspirator
at Poona, the Wahabee high priest and disciples in

[1] Colonel Ovans was deputed from Satara to Kolapoor, in the
insurrection of 1844–45. The circumstances of his capture were
curious, though for the time critical. The relays of bearers posted
for him were carried off by the rebels, and others substituted for
them, who, acting to all appearance as his own people, carried him
in the dead of night to the neighbouring Fort of Punalla, where he
narrowly escaped the bursting of our bomb-shells when we afterwards took the place.

[2] Adopted sons of the ex- and of the lately deceased Rajas of
Satara.

the Southern Mahratta Country, some of whom were in the 27th Regiment, Native Infantry, at Kolapoor.

Ill fortune continued to pursue me on my way to Satara; my carriage twice came to grief, once in a nulla, where the stream poured into it. It was night and raining hard, and my last relay of horses became so dead beat as not to be able to go faster than a mile or two an hour. On arrival I found good news had just been received by telegraph from Kolapoor of the defeat of a party of the mutineers, and that affairs wore a less gloomy appearance. There was no road from Satara to Kolapoor beyond the ordinary fair-weather track, and black soil nearly the whole way in which during the monsoon horses frequently sank to their girths, and carriage-wheels to the axles; besides which there were several large rivers and minor streams now of course unfordable, and all unbridged.

Time being everything, I pushed on two guns with double allowance of men and horses, leaving the remainder to await return of means of transport;

the dragoons I did not take, partly owing to the difficulty of the march for heavily-mounted men, and partly from the conviction that whatever work I had to do would be done before they could join me, as I pushed on myself with a few men of the Southern Mahratta Horse,[1] and reached Kolapoor just before midnight, August 14, putting up at the hospitable residence of the Political Superintendent, Colonel Maughan, where during the crisis the European community had been sheltered.

All was dark as to the origin and extent of the conspiracy. Colonel Maughan knew only that traitorous correspondence had been going on between the regiment and the town, and with Belgaum, and intercepted letters showed proceedings in the latter place of formidable and extensive character, but the evidence reached no nearer than to secondary parties and go-betweens.

For two days I was employed examining, individually and collectively, every officer, European

[1] A capital body of light horsemen, a detachment of which had just distinguished itself greatly in a march under command of Lieut. Kerr, made without halting from Satara to Kolapoor, a distance of seventy miles.

and Native, of the Regiment, and others, without obtaining any clue to the causes of discontent, or explanation of the extraordinary conduct of the men ; not one would or could admit the existence of any grievance, or assign any reason for the out-break. It appeared that the night of the mutiny, July 31, after plundering *ad lib.* at the station, the greater portion of the regiment proceeded to the town, expecting to be taken in, but Colonel Maughan had secured the closing of the gates before their arrival, and whatever may have been the understanding that took them thither, it had not been sufficient to procure a movement in their favour inside, whereupon two hundred odd took up their quarters in the Paga, a small outwork adjoining the town, where the Raja's horses, menagerie, &c., were kept, and the remainder returned to their lines. Colonel Maughan, with the Kolapoor Local Infantry only, there being no other force at the station, marched against them, but was received by a volley of musketry, and found the position too strong to assail with any chance of success with untried soldiers and no artillery. He himself was slightly wounded, and, all things considered, was fully justified in retiring.

The next day the mutineers left the Paga, and marched off, apparently to join their comrades at Rutnagherry, but on descending the Ghats they found the road blocked by the landing of European soldiers sent by sea from Bombay. This had been done for the first time I believe in Indian history, as it was previously considered a thing impossible to land on that coast during the height of the monsoon, Bombay and Goa being, during that season, the only ports available.[1] Checked in this way, the greater number of the mutineers, under command of a Sawunt Waree leader, one Ramjee Sirsat, betook themselves to the Waree jungles, where the insurgents in 1844–45 had given such trouble, and about forty, all Purdesees (Hindostan men), returned to Kolapoor, and reoccupied the Paga. Here they were attacked, August 10, by volunteers from their own regiment, Lieutenant Kerr's detach-

[1] The services of the Indian Navy during the rebellion are beyond praise. They deserved a better reward than its abolition after the danger had passed away. The good of India seems to have been little consulted in this measure.

ment of S. M. Horse, whose splendid march I have alluded to, some of the artillery borrowed from the town, nearly useless, and some of the Local Corps, all under Major Rolland, the Commanding Officer of the 27th. The balls, being much too small for the cannon, hit anywhere except the point aimed at, but a private entrance having been pointed out to Lieutenant Kerr,[1] he got in unperceived till he reached the interior buildings, where a desperate conflict ensued; Lieutenant Innes, with a party of the 27th, at the same time taking the mutineers in the rear, the whole number were either killed or taken prisoners, fighting to the last, only a few surviving, and those almost all wounded. This affair had, I found, restored some degree of confidence in the mutinous regiment, and the officers had returned to their houses. I was sorely puzzled to account for the mutiny at all, since no cause could be discovered, but the very concealment on the part of the whole regiment bore a suspicious aspect, for such an outbreak

[1] Lieut. Kerr afterwards received the V. C., and Lieut. Innes a staff appointment, for their services on this occasion.

could not have occurred without some preliminary movements and exciting causes ; and that the mutineers should so long have hugged the town showed expectation of support therefrom ; why none was given was a mystery not solved for some months afterwards.

To enable the reader to understand the position of affairs, it is necessary to give a brief abstract of the previous history of Kolapoor. This State and the adjoining one of Satara were bequeathed by Siwajee, founder of the Mahratta empire, to his two sons, the younger receiving Kolapoor. The discussions in England that followed the displacement of the then Raja of Satara in favour of a younger brother must be generally known; and the wakeel of the former, Rungo Bapoojee by name, may be remembered as advocating in London for some years his master's claims. On the decease of the younger brother we took possession, refusing to recognise the adopted son of either prince, and thereby uniting against us the supporters of both ; of which Rungo Bapoojee took advantage, and in conjunction with Nana Sahib became a leading conspirator in 1857–58. The conspiracies in Western India first came to light at Satara through the exertions of Mr. Rose and his able Assistants, and were there nipped in the bud by the deportation of the two princes before alluded to, and the execution of sundry conspirators; one, a son of Rungo Bapoojee, was seized in Kolapoor, sent to Satara, and there tried and executed. Although a reward was offered for the apprehension of his father, he disappeared and has never since been heard of.

To return to Kolapoor. The Raja who died in 1842, left two sons, both children, one a few days older than the other; whereupon our Government assumed the management, appointing a native employé as minister, who was to act under the control of the Political Agent at Belgaum. Both sons, perhaps on the '*divide et impera*' principle, were treated alike, and we seized the opportunity to introduce such reforms into the State as were advantageous to our own interests *if not to it*, but on this point opinions might naturally differ. The Durbar disliked our abolition of the old hereditary

garrisons of their forts, of which they had many
very strong ones.   These garrisons were composed
of a class of men called Gudkurres (lit. fort keepers),
established by the great Siwajee.   All the lands
surrounding the forts were held by them on tenure
of service therein.   Our measures on that occasion
had led to the insurrection of 1844–45, which took
a force of upwards of ten thousand men nine
months to quell above and below the Ghats, where
the Sawunt Waree people joined in the rebellion.
It ended in the appointment of a separate Political
Superintendent at Kolapoor over our native minister,
and the deportation of the dowager Ranee, who was
believed to have fomented the intrigues.   The
whole of the expenses incurred in suppressing this
outbreak were charged to the Kolapoor and Sawunt
Waree States. in the proportion of two-thirds to
the one, and one-third to the other, with five per
cent. interest until repaid ; and as under our more
expensive system of management, repayment in
either case appeared nearly hopeless, the conviction
gained ground that native rule was never to be

restored,[1] and as a consequence all adherents of native dynasties naturally favoured the intrigues of the time.

I was fully conscious of the state of public feeling, but all my efforts to pierce beneath the surface failed, so true were all to each other; and there was little but suspicion and conjecture to go on; but the reports of the various agents I employed, of different classes unknown to each other, convinced me, more by the little I could ascertain, than from what was actually said, that we could thoroughly depend on none, for disaffection was general. In the former rebellion I had been placed in charge of the Sawunt Waree district, six years' residence in which gave me some influence over its people, and rendered the politics of this part of India not altogether new to me, and I had hoped to have sounded the depth of the present outbreak through those whose confidence I had

[1] On the marriage of the elder Raja with the daughter of the Gaekwar, the latter is reported to have endeavoured to secure the restoration of power to his son-in-law, by offering to guarantee payment of the debt. I am not aware of the reasons given for our refusal, but it convinced the Kolapoor family of the hopelessness of their case.

M

then gained, one of whom, a leading Sirdar, was connected by marriage with the Kolapoor Durbar. Kolapoor is the principal State of the Southern Mahratta country. It has a population not far short of a million, and a net revenue of about ten lakhs, with as much more of alienated lands, jageers, &c. Numerous other smaller States remained under the control of the Political Agent at Belgaum, my authority being limited to Kolapoor and Sawunt Waree, with command of all the troops, regular and irregular, there and at Rutnagherry.

My force in Europeans and in artillery was far too weak to authorise more than the most circumspect action, watching events and endeavouring to ascertain the real cause of the mutiny. Three days after my own arrival, the two horse-artillery guns came in, and about a hundred of the 2nd European Regiment from the coast: such a spectacle it was painful to see. The men had marched through deep mud and torrents of rain, across swollen streams, and such of their kit as they had managed to bring was ruined. The horse artillery, coming by the upper road, arrived in better condition. A body of workmen had been employed under an engineer officer in laying down branches of trees where the mud was deepest, to prevent the wheels sinking so far, and otherwise facilitating their progress.

Owing to the general complicity of the regiment the night of the outbreak, and the impossibility experienced by the officers of finding any help in their efforts to restore order, I felt it impossible to draw a line between the different shades of criminality, or, if innocent, of cowardice, in the body. Without entering into my reasons for rejecting as a criterion the assistance rendered in attacking their comrades in the Paga, it will be enough to say here what was subsequently proved, that some of the foremost on that occasion were amongst the worst of the mutineers. One fact shall be mentioned to show the difficulty of dealing with such a people. Only four or five days after the outbreak, a Subadar (native captain) had made himself conspicuous by seizing a messenger from the town, who came to him on the part of a person of some note residing there, a Mohammedan gentleman late from Baroda, with a message of enquiry as to mutual co-operation, and promise of support. This emissary was at once tried, convicted, and executed ; yet this very subadar was afterwards proved to have been one of the leaders of the mutiny, and, after long and careful trial, was condemned and executed.

The difficulty of sifting the innocent from the guilty, and the danger of lending too ready an ear to plausible accusations, cannot be better shown than by an incident that occurred during my investigations.

The daughter of the Gaekwar coming from Baroda to join her husband, with a considerable retinue, had passed through Poona on her way to Kolapoor. Just before she arrived at the latter place, Mr. Rose, the magistrate of Satara, sent me word that he had received information inducing him to believe that the Ranee's party had held interviews with suspected persons at Poona, and had been intrusted with a communication to co-conspirators in Kolapoor which I should do well to intercept. I took measures accordingly, and my trusted aide, Captain John Schneider, observed a man on finding himself caught putting something in his mouth which he endeavoured hastily to swallow. He was at once seized, and a partly-chewed paper drawn from his throat, which proved to be a letter of a highly treasonable character from certain parties at Poona to the confidential attendant of the Ranee's husband, the elder Raja.

The bearer would only admit that he had been asked to deliver the letter, and that he had attempted to swallow it, fearing it might possibly bring him into trouble. Of course all those so implicated were secured, for at such a time an event of this kind afforded strong presumption of guilt ; but the result of a most searching enquiry proved that they were innocent, and that the whole thing was a *ruse* to throw me off the scent, and perhaps to injure some whose friendliness to the rebel cause was suspected.

It was a serious question whether or not, with so few Europeans present, to disarm the regiment without delay. On one hand was the danger of the men rising to attack us before our force gathered strength, or of marching away with their arms, as so many had already done; also the danger of allowing them time to brood over what might follow on our strength increasing, reinforcements being always magnified by native rumour. On the other hand, if I disarmed at once, lay the risk of our small number tempting them to resist, and I had no means then of knowing what dependence might be placed on the Local Corps. It was a balance of risks and of probabilities, and on the whole it appeared to me advisable at once to disarm, notwithstanding the warnings from Lord Elphinstone to be cautious and wait for strength.

My force consisted of two guns, horse artillery, two howitzers, mountain train, twenty-five men, under Captain (now Colonel) Sealy; about ninety men, 2nd European Light Infantry, under Colonel Guerin; one hundred and eighty S. M. Horse, under Lieut. Kerr, and about three hundred and fifty Kolapoor Local Infantry, commanded by Captain John Schneider; amply sufficient if the native portion proved faithful.

On the day for the disarming parade, August 18,

I drew up the Europeans with the Kolapoor Local Corps in one line, loaded the guns with grape and canister, and at a right angle to these the S. M. Horse; in the space thus commanded, the mutinous regiment was formed in quarter-distance column. Calling Commanders to the front, I told them that I should address the Regiment in words that I trusted would come home to their hearts, and that I had every hope no resistance would be attempted to the deprivation of their arms; but that, should I be disappointed, I would give the sound by bugle, when they were to direct one round from each gun, and one volley from each corps, taking what care they might to avoid shooting the European Officers of the 27th, and my staff as we retired upon them. The cavalry were then to sweep along the whole front of the line, and 'You, Lieutenant Kerr,' I added, addressing him, 'will, I know, leave little for the Judge Advocate to do, for an example will be specially necessary, this being the first Regiment of our army that has caught the contagion from their treacherous brethren in Bengal.'

It was an anxious moment, for hundreds of these men of the 27th knew they were standing with halters round their necks, and the boldest spirits among them might have been tempted to make a struggle for life before they were quite at my mercy. I then addressed them, appealing to every motive that could lead them to reproach themselves for, and regret their conduct, at the same time giving them assurance that none would be punished but those on whom guilt might be proved after fair trial.

'It must be evident to you,' I continued, 'that Government cannot trust with arms a body of their soldiers who, on a mutinous explosion in the regiment, failed to support their Officers, allowed the public treasure-chest in their charge to be broken open and its contents carried off, the shops in the bazaar plundered, not only without any attempt at resistance, but as yet without a single individual coming forward to say by whom all this was done; nor have any of you given me the slightest clue to the cause of the mutiny, nor mentioned any grievance that accounts for it. The wheat, therefore, must be separated from the chaff by strict enquiry, if wheat there be, before confidence can be regained and the arms restored. But, as many of you have shown fidelity during the late attack on the Paga, I am willing to hope the best, and will not therefore disgrace all by depriving you of military symbols; until further orders the ramrod may be used at parade and on guard instead of the musket, and the native officers may retain their swords. The regiment will attend parades and do other duty as may be directed.'

Before I had finished speaking I observed tears on the faces of some of the front rank close to me. These native soldiers are but children of a larger growth. The order was then given to pile arms, obedience to which was the crucial part of the proceedings; that once done, all was safe. After a slight but ominous pause they obeyed, and the column being filed off to the flank, all danger was over. The arms were then taken possession of, and parties detached to disarm the several guards, and to search the mens' lines for anything sus-picious there might be, a Native Officer of the 27th accompanying each party to see that due respect was paid to families. Of course it was not to be expected, with so many days given for concealment, that anything important would be found ; the few in whose huts suspicious articles were discovered were taken into custody, and the remainder, when all was over, marched back to their lines. Courts-martial, European and Native, were told off for the trial of such prisoners as were forthcoming under the new law just passed (Act 14 of 1857), empowering commanders of stations and forces to convene such and carry out their sentences, whether of life or death, at discretion.

To show the difficulties met with in these trials I give the case of one individual. In the general spoliation that took place the night of the mutiny, a goldsmith in the bazaar recognised one of those who broke into his house, from having had previous dealings with him, and the man was therefore secured and tried for mutiny as the graver offence. The native court-martial acquitted him of this charge on evidence of alibi, but as the goldsmith continued positive, and previous intercourse tendered it most unlikely that he was mistaken, this, with other circumstances, led me shortly after to try the prisoner again before an European court-martial, on a charge of burglary, when he was again acquitted, the bazaar guard of the night swearing to his being present with them the whole time, and never having left the guard-house. Ulti-mately he was discharged when the regiment was disbanded, and on the preparation of the lines for their successors of the 15th N.I., the goldsmith's valuables were found buried under the suspected man's fireplace. There was no doubt that that part of the guard's evidence was true, wherein they stated that he had never left them, for they were all engaged plundering together, but no evidence to convict them could be obtained.

The 27th being retained on the Roster for duty, its Native Officers sat with those of the other corps on the courts, and as enquiry went slowly forward, and the truth came gradually to light, many who had sat in judgment and condemned their fellows, were themselves tried, convicted, and executed. Of course there was no difficulty in proving the

guilt of those made prisoners in the attack on the
Paga. Altogether twenty-one on the day following the disarmament were convicted, and the whole
of the troops assembled that same afternoon to
carry out the sentences ; four of the Raja's guns
being borrowed for the purpose.

I will not enter into the details of this terrible
scene. Eight were blown from guns, two hung,
and eleven shot by musketry.[1] All met death

---

[1] The painful nature of this part of the tragedy was heightened
by an incident that shows the routine character of our departmental
systems.

Of the unhappy victims of retribution sentenced to die by musketry, some after the first volley were untouched, whilst others
remained writhing at their stakes more or less wounded. The
cartridges furnished to the Europeans proved to be the same that I
had protested against when endeavouring to arm the Light Battalion
with Enfields for the Persian campaign.

I had received permission to select a hundred, and on visiting the
Grand Arsenal for the purpose, found numbers of men making up
cartridges for them with the iron cup that experience in Europe
had condemned. On pointing this out to the Principal Commissary
of Ordnance, he replied that he knew nothing of the experiments
that had led to the rejection of the cup at home ; that if true, it was
a matter for others to see to ; his business was to use the cup since it
had been sent out from England for the new cartridges, and if I
disliked them I had better get the head of the Military Board to
interfere. To him accordingly I went, and was then answered, ' I
have read of the experiments you allude to, but nothing has come
before me officially on the subject, therefore I can take no action to
prevent the cartridges from being made up with the cup.' I then

with fortitude, refusing to purchase life by betraying their common secret. One man badly wounded, and brought in a litter to the ground, shook off the artillerymen who were lifting him to the gun, burst his bandages, and walked forward with an air of proud defiance. I felt great compassion for him, and, as I passed along the line, stopped and told him how it grieved me to see so fine a soldier in this miserable condition. 'But you must know,' I said, 'that you have been faithless to your salt, and brought on yourself a just punishment. You cannot have so acted without some strong motive, and in obedience to some one or more in higher position, who have misled you. Only promise to tell the whole truth, and you shall be at once untied from the gun and your life spared.'

wrote to the Adjutant-General of the army, describing the mischief going forward, and received the reply that the subject would be attended to. I had suddenly to embark for the Gulf of Persia without my Enfields, and now, so long afterwards, it appeared that these very cup cartridges had just been served out in Bombay to our European soldiery sent on a dangerous service, where they might have been as units to hundreds. This first day of trial, the lead of several remained in the barrels, the cup blowing through, hitting or missing the condemned. Of course the march in that severe weather had increased the inefficiency of the firing parties from dampness of powder and caps.

He looked at me with a scowl and smile mingled, and answered, 'What I have done I have done,' then turned his head away, and remained silent.

Fifty-one men thus met their death at different periods as the trials went on, before a Sepoy, as I passed down the line of guns on September 9,[1] replied, in answer to my appeal, 'I only obeyed the orders of Subadar Daood Beg.' He was immediately untied and ordered to be strictly confined, and kept from communication with anyone.

Thus was the first dawn of light thrown upon the conspiracy in the regiment. The man did not know much, but his evidence showed that the ferment of mutiny had been brewing long, that more or less of the Native Officers were implicated, besides the one named, that many were in constant correspondence with Bengal, and that it was understood among the men that the obnoxious cartridge

[1] The day before this parade, the road *viâ* Satara to Bombay being now thought safe, the ladies took flight with a small escort. Mrs. John Schneider alone remained with her husband, as much from inherent courage, displayed throughout this trying period, as from confidence in the fidelity of his corps.

was to be issued to them. A detail from the corps had been sent, in common with many others, to the School of Musketry at Poona, to learn the new drill, whence one of them wrote that 'they had bitten the fatal cartridge,' and asked what was to be their fate! This became a subject of anxious conversation in the regiment. The Subadar-major, an old veteran entitled to his pension, on being questioned about it by a Sepoy, replied with a shrug, 'What can be done? there is no contending against fate ; and you know it has been predicted we are all to become of one caste!' Nothing afterwards transpired to implicate him in the conspiracy further than the fact of his keeping his European Officers in ignorance of the feeling of the regiment. As another illustration of this feeling, worked up by seditious intriguers, I give the case of a deserter from the 27th on the night of the mutiny, who was subsequently caught in his own village. On being questioned as to the reason of his not joining his officers, he replied, 'Where was I to go? All the world said the English Raj had come to an end, and so, being a quiet man, I thought the best place to take refuge in was my own home.'

I could not proceed to trial on the unsupported evidence of an accomplice, yet I felt justified in making prisoners of Subadar Daood Beg, and a few others prominently named; and some time elapsed before the confessions of one prisoner after another gave me further stepping-stones towards unravelling the mystery. Whenever this happened, the parties were kept completely separated, so as to admit of no possibility of intercommunication, and the confessions being thus made, agreement as to facts and persons became of the nature of judicial proof.

It was not till after events yet to be related that I found out how it was that the regiment had been deceived in its hopes of admission into the town on the night of the mutiny. The plan of the joint conspirators had been to rise on the 10th of August, and that day was therefore given out as the one on which the new cartridge was to be issued.[1] But the native adjutant, a Jew, was dis-

[1] One of the leading mutineers was the Quarter-master Havildar, who, being in charge of the arms and ammunition in store, knew

trusted in the regiment, and when, on July 31, it was discovered that he was sending away his family, whose presence was regarded as a security for his fidelity, if not for his co-operation, it was taken as a sign that he was about to betray them. After dusk that evening, some of the leaders held a council, whereat an additional motive for prompt action was brought forward, for, through a native employé in the telegraph office, it had leaked out that European soldiers were being sent from Bombay It was decided to rise at once, but this having been done without concert with the town, our chief functionary there had been able to keep the gates closed.

well that not a single rifle or cartridge was at the station, or even expected, hereby proving that the dread of this new caste-destroyer was made use of by the prime movers of the great revolt as a fulcrum for their lever.

CHAPTER XI.

THE FIRST OUTBREAK OF REBELLION.

THE state of the country meanwhile grew more unsettled. Vague rumours reached me of intended risings, but none could be traced to rest on any sufficient foundation, beyond the fact that there was a common sense of coming disturbance.

The cause that led the mutinous regiment to expect help from the town, and to cling to it so pertinaciously, yet remained unsolved. None of the Political Agent's establishment, up to the minister residing therein, who had closed the gates the night of the mutiny, seemed conscious of anything wrong on the part of the Durbar, or in the country.

All that could be done was to watch and wait. By the end of October the uneasiness was reported by my scouts to have become so general that I felt it right for the whole force to sleep under arms, the unarmed 27th regiment to be diligently watched, and all things to be in preparation to turn out, especially after nightfall, at a moment's notice. On November 15th the elder Raja called on the Political Agent to acquaint him that he had heard of an intention to attack our camp; but, as he stated this on mere rumour, not knowing if it were true, nor giving any clue to trace its origin, he was only bringing coals to Newcastle. Had his brother been our informant, I should at once have suspected a *ruse*, but the elder prince was indolent, quiet, and inoffensive, not likely to join in, or perhaps be trusted in any intrigue. The younger brother, Chimma Sahib, on the contrary, was a man of energy, a true descendant of Siwaji, and highly popular in the country.

I took the precaution of increasing my patrols and picquets, and ordering certain sentries to mount loaded. Happily the European force had been somewhat increased both from Belgaum and Rutnagerry. So matters remained until December 4. That afternoon, as I was sitting facing the entrance doorway, I observed a young man expostulating with the peon in waiting outside, and finding he wished to speak to me, directed his admission. On entering, he threw himself at my feet, saying: 'Sir, I have something to communicate to you in private.' As he was unarmed, and I liked the expression of his face, I took him apart, when he informed me that he had just left a body of insurgents, who had secretly gathered, to the number of five hundred, in the jungle of a village ten miles off; that he understood their purpose was to attack my camp; that he had left them on the plea of obtaining his parents' permission to join them; accordingly he said, 'I have come to you, as the Sirkar is my ma-bap' (literally, Government is my mother and father). I laughed, and replied, 'Surely the people are not such fools as to beard the lion in his den.' 'It's no laughing matter, Sahib,' he answered, 'what I say is true.' Further conversation convinced me he was in earnest; I therefore persuaded him to go back with a couple of my scouts, whom he could pass off as volunteers joining with himself; these were directed to return with all the information they could acquire.

The next day all three reappeared, confirming the intelligence; but as the name of the leader or leaders had remained concealed, they were sent back at once if possible to obtain it. They had found the insurgents in scattered groups concealed amongst the trees, their supplies being furnished from the neighbouring village, but none would say who had brought them together.

In the extreme uncertainty of the real feeling of the native soldiery, and of the whole country, and with much reason to suspect both, I had from the first thought it best to show no distrust, and therefore employed no guard during the day, and for night only a small party from the Local Infantry, for one sentry in the front of the house, and some half-dozen of the Durbar men for another in the rear; but I slept with a battery of small arms under my pillow and around my head. That same night, or rather about 2 A.M., I was aroused by the near clatter of horses' feet. Pistols in belt, I rushed to the doorway, and found that it was the Rissaldar in command of the S. M. Horse, who informed me that his picquets had brought word of suspicious cries in the town, and that no reply was given from a gateway guard when challenged; he had therefore at once made his men fall in, and brought them to me for orders. I directed him to sweep round the town, sound all the gates, ending with the main one on the road leading to the camp, where I should be found collecting the troops, and would expect his report. If he could gain admittance, he was to hold one entrance.

This man, Rehman Khan, was a fine old warrior, who, when a lad, had fought on our side in 1817–18 against the Peishwa. He was a born cavalry soldier. On Lieutenant Kerr's departure with a hundred men of the S. M. Horse to watch the frontier of the Nizam's dominions, where trouble was apprehended, he became senior officer, and proved very efficient.

Sending tidings of what had occurred to the Civil Lines, and orders as to the movement of the Local Corps, I galloped into camp, and sounded the alarm.

To provide for the worst, I had long before prepared a place of rendezvous at a quadrangular building used originally for the gun bullocks, &c. of the artillery. This I had loopholed and traversed, so that anything but an artillery attack might be resisted, and here all non-combatants were to assemble for protection when the alarm sounded. Until I received the Rissaldar's report, I could form no plan of operations, but I had not to wait long before a message was sent that he had sounded every gateway and been denied access, but had not been fired upon—that the place was apparently in hostile possession, and that he had taken up his position between the camp and town, in front of the main gateway, as ordered. As every gate had thus fallen into the enemy's hands without opposition—for not a shot had been heard —it was evident that the armed force of the town were either themselves rebels, or in league with them. That this could be without connivance of the Durbar seemed most improbable, and I therefore drew the inference that the rebel gathering outside had intended an attack on my camp, at the same time that their friends rose in the town, so that my attention being distracted, the town folk might have time to arrange their plans.

Kolapoor was a fortified city, so strong that whenever, in former years, we had occasion to threaten it, a force of many thousand men with a siege train always took the field; the gateways were especially formidable, offering to assailants a fire in front, flank, and rear. With my little force, not two hundred Europeans of all ranks, my only chance of success was to take it by surprise.

To wait for the threatened attack would have been to shut out this chance. As a choice of evils, therefore, I gave up, for the time, the protection of the cantonments, the rendezvous excepted, for the defence of which I left a trusty non-commissioned officer of the 2nd Europeans with twenty men, and orders to defend his post to the last extremity. Mrs. Guerin, who had recently joined her husband, came to take shelter here just as I was leaving, and hearing my instructions, cried to me, 'I can trust our men—we will never surrender!'

Mrs. Schneider, also confiding in her husband's corps, took shelter with the family of the senior native officer.

With the rendezvous safe, nothing more was to be feared than loss from destruction of property, and danger from the effect of this upon the country; but an opportunity of securing the town once lost, months might elapse before sufficient force could be assembled to regain it, and meanwhile its being in possession of the rebels might tempt them everywhere to rise. The great difficulty was how to deal with the 27th N. I., whom I could not take with me, and did not like to leave behind. Doubtless many would have volunteered for service, as they had done before, but from the experience since gained, it was impossible to trust them, and I could not help fearing some secret relation between them, or some of them, and the rebels outside. I therefore directed their formation on their own parade-ground, there to await orders, and meanwhile to be allowed as much liberty, under the eyes of their officers, as was consistent with surveillance; a mounted officer to gallop with a report to me of anything creating alarm.

Ordering a powder-bag to be made up, I detached fifty Europeans, under two active and intelligent officers, Lieutenants Stanley Scott and Jervis, to the main gateway, to join the Rissaldar's party, with orders to get in by skilful management if possible. If opposed, they were not to incur needless loss, as the gate was far too strong to force, but to keep up a show of attack to distract attention. With the remainder of the force I marched to the rear of the town, passing near to the Civil Lines, where Captain John Schneider and his corps joined me. The telegraph office being found deserted, I left messages and people to hunt for the frightened clerks, and moved on to the attack, just previous to which I received the consoling intelligence that the wires were cut, and it was not for some time after that I discovered this to be a mistake, an obstruction only having occurred, which they were able to remove. This delay may perhaps account for the confused way in which my telegrams were published in Bombay.

Day dawned just before we reached the gateway. Time being everything, and the powder-bag not up, I ordered Lieutenant Holberton, an active and zealous officer commanding the artillery, to blow in the gate. The bridge over the ditch was too narrow to admit of more than one of the six pounders being brought up at a time. A hot-tempered young soldier, in his anxious haste, put the cartridge in shot foremost, and several caps were snapped in vain. Happily for us, the rebels were not prepared for our attacking that gate, for with a handful of resolute men against us, few on our side would have lived to tell the tale. During this awkward pause, I observed by my side Dr. Broughton, surgeon of the Agency, who was always to the front where danger was expected or work to be done. 'Doctor,' I said, 'you had better go under cover, or who will there be to cut off arms and legs when we are bowled over?' 'Who will there be to apply a tourniquet if I go? A stitch in time saves nine!' was his rejoinder, nor was mere persuasion sufficient to induce him to retire. The gun had to be run back over the crowded narrow causeway to allow the other to come up, in which process my zealous staff-officer, Captain Thompson, was knocked into the ditch, horse and all, happily with no serious hurt ; the other gun was rapidly brought up, and just as Sergeant Pain arrived with the powder-bag, the gate was forced open, and the storming party rushed in. There were scarcely a dozen rebels near the gateway, and these, as we entered, fled, firing random shots.

I detached parties right and left to scour the ramparts, with orders to fire only when fired upon, lest the inhabitants might needlessly suffer ; and with the rest proceeded to take the main gateway in the rear, and perhaps save the jail close to it from falling into rebel hands. Besides the usual classes of such a domicile, it contained between thirty and forty convict mutineers, detained there preparatory to transportation, who would have made a formidable accession of strength to the enemy. During these operations, altogether only eight rebels were killed, and two men of Captain Schneider's corps wounded.

Before advancing, I heard shots in the centre of the town, hereafter to be explained. The rebels finding themselves taken in flank and rear, and, as it turned out, their leader killed, lost heart; except a few, who rushed upon the storming party, they dispersed in all directions, and we took possession of the main gate, through which only the artillery could easily enter, and reached the jail in time to prevent mischief. This was mainly due to the fidelity and good conduct of the Nazir, who had closed the outer gates, kept the prisoners safe, and turned a deaf ear to the entreaties and threats of the rebels.

We were now in possession of the place, and of the chief avenue to the Palace. This is quite a royal residence; the building forms three sides of a square or rather parallelogram, closed by a low wall—the road entering the court by a handsome arched gateway. What was the state of things within, it was impossible to guess, but if hostile it was itself a fortress needing the utmost circumspection before attack. Captain Schneider volunteered to go with a white flag, as my herald, to ascertain particulars, and deliver my terms. These were—arms to be surrendered, and, in general, readiness to accede to what I might consider it necessary to do, with the promise of protection to all not found concerned in the insurrection, and respect to the honour and feelings of the royal family. I had none with me so competent to the task as he, and so likely to succeed in staying further bloodshed, else I should have scrupled to send, on what appeared so hazardous a service, one who was my right arm both in civil and military work.

During his absence the scattered parties came in with their prisoners, and all was made safe for permanent occupation and defence inside of the main gateway. After a painful half-hour of suspense Capt. Schneider returned. He had found the Palace filled with hundreds of armed men, crowded on roofs, windows, and every available standing-place. A dead body was lying near a small field-piece near the centre of the square. He went forward with his single attendant and demanded an interview with the Rajas, which was at once conceded. Nothing was said or done to explain the assembly of such an armed force, nor why, being there, they should have allowed the gates to be quietly taken possession of. Both Rajas consented to my terms, the elder expressing gratitude for Captain Schneider's visit. It was stated that the rebels had taken the town by escalade. The firing we had heard, when at the gateway, proved to have been from a small party of his own corps, in charge of the treasure-chest kept in the Palace buildings, who reported that the rebels, having brought a gun in front, had threatened to fire unless the Rajas surrendered, and that having heard my cannon at the gateway, they had fired at them for answer, and fortunately killed their leader, after which the insurgents left, but some in the Palace had abused the local corps for what they had done, and all but themselves had remained passive.

On receiving this report we marched into the Palace square and the disarmament began. A large drum covered by a flag, being placed in the centre, the prisoners, up to this time taken, were then and there tried by drum-head court-martial,[1] under an old and experienced officer, Col. Guerin, as President, who soon reported that concerning thirty-six there was no doubt, and that these had moreover pleaded guilty; but as the remainder pleaded not guilty, and evidence on both sides had to be fully gone into, the day might pass before they could arrive at a verdict ; therefore thirty-six only were then tried and the rest removed for subsequent procedure.   These thirty-six being convicted and condemned to death, I carried out the sentence on the spot, along the wall fronting the Palace, feeling convinced that most of those inside were as guilty as these poor creatures, and that a stern example was needed to convince all of the folly of armed opposition to our Government, the more especially as this, like the previous mutinous outbreak, was the first of its kind in Western India.

Painful as the work was, I felt certain that

[1] Indian Government Acts, 8, 11, 14 and 16 of May—June 57, had much to do with the speedy suppression of the general rebellion, whenever they were promptly availed of.   In its earlier stages the Western Presidency had this great advantage over Bengal, where revolt became formidable before these Acts were published.

severity now would be mercy in the end. The insurgents who had got into the town were, so far as I could ascertain, not more than two hundred. They had evidently come on an understanding that they would receive support from within. A portion of them consisted of the hereditary garrison of Punalla, whose leader was now executed. Unhappily I could then obtain no clue to enable me to lay hands on the prime movers of the mischief; suspicion strongly pointed to the younger Raja; but being unwilling to act without some proof, I contented myself with a firm grip of the place, a strong European guard at the main gateway, loaded cannon commanding the approaches, and guards from the local corps at all the smaller gates. This corps, equally with the S.M. Horse, had behaved well throughout, and furnished half the firing party for the executions. The disarming of the town could now go safely forward.

In my interview with the two Rajas, the elder repeated his expressions of gratitude, the younger remaining silent; whereupon I told them that but

for the administration resting with ourselves, and
our own appointed minister being the authorised
party to exact obedience, I should have held them
responsible for the misconduct of their men in
offering no opposition to the rebels.   This minister
was an old Government servant, selected for the
office, and why he was so helpless remains a mystery, but as he had closed the gates against the
mutinous regiment, I had thought it right to
continue trusting him.

The heavy work of the day over, something to
break our fast was ordered from camp, the men,
who had been many hours under arms, were allowed
to pile them, and we all fell to.

This being seen from the palace windows, the
Ranees sent us dishes of pillaos and choice things,
and hunger joined to the tempting odour, overcame
the '*timeo Danaos*, &c.,' misgivings of some.   Had
we been aware of a scene then enacting in the
Palace, we might not have enjoyed the fare so well.
Long afterwards I was informed that while thus
occupied, Chimma Sahib and a few confidential
adherents were closeted together.   ' See,' said a Sir-

dar, who himself had fifty followers,[1] 'it is not yet too late; these grasping foreigners are off their guard and the men's arms piled; give but the word and we will make a sudden rush and cut them to pieces before they can rally.' Whether this was mere bravado or not it was considered too hazardous, and happily for us was not attempted, for I must confess, that I was thrown off my guard by the turn events had taken, and the sentries might have been suddenly cut down.

In the afternoon we marched back to camp. The reports from time to time received from it had been satisfactory, and no attack attempted. The informer and scouts had returned to the rebel rendezvous that night and found the birds flown; they understood from a few stragglers left behind, that one party had gone off to the town, and another to the camp. They came back as I was forcing my way through the gate, and had therefore no means of communicating their information until the hurley-burley was over. I concluded

[1] This man, like a true Mahratta, had been the first to meet me with the offer of his sword and services to lull suspicion.

that, as the firing of the guns proved we were on the alert, the party intending the attack on the camp had considered discretion the better part of valour, and retreated, but it is possible that the whole thing was a *ruse* in order to distract my attention from the intended work in the town, the intriguers likewise employing the Raja to throw me off the scent. In this case he may have been an unconscious tool, for nothing in the course of my proceedings criminated him.

However this may be, there is no doubt that our prompt seizure of the town whilst Chimma Sahib was still wavering, prevented the execution of a plot from whose evil consequences to himself, if unsuccessful, he might hope to escape by the plea of coercion. Precisely this dodge, attempted by one of the Southern Mahratta chiefs, was frustrated by Captain Frederick Schneider, who, in pursuit of a party of Sawunt rebels, came suddenly on their bivouack, and, amongst other things left in the hurry of their flight, picked up fragments of a letter, which put together proved to be from the said chief to the rebel leader, the noted Baba

Desae, promising to join him on condition of being seemingly carried off by force.

From this time trials of the civil rebels went on *pari passu* with those of the military, and each class of cases served to throw light on the other.

Thus among the military there were the Mohammedan element and the Hindoo element, separate, and yet both joining in and making the issue of the greased cartridge to the School of Musketry at Poona an instrument to excite alarm and discontent. But no evidence could be obtained except from those who gave it to save their lives, which always rendered it more or less suspicious.

At one execution parade for some of the insurgents taken in the town, I was sent for by the officer commanding, to say that one of them had offered to tell the truth if pardoned, and he therefore awaited orders. Although the horse artilleryman who brought me the message had come at a gallop, and I returned with equal speed, there had been time for mischief.

The man was one of the petty leaders, and when tied to the gun had named an officer of the Raja's body-guard as the person whose instructions he had complied with, believing them to come from the Durbar. An escort of this troop had brought the prisoners from the jail to the parade ground, and unfortunately remained near enough to hear the name mentioned. It was remembered afterwards that one of the party had cantered off[1] in the direction of the town, and although I lost not a moment in sending trustworthy men to seize the officer implicated, they were too late. I offered a considerable reward for his apprehension, but he was never found.

Still, though collusion was evident, I could get no proof of it, and the fidelity with which all parties adhered to each other was marvellous. The disarming of the country meanwhile went forward. Out of courtesy I allowed the Rajas to retain sufficient arms for their ordinary attendants and for themselves.

European reinforcements now reached both Bel-

---

[1] When this was enquired into, the plea was assigned of something forgotten ; it was therefore plain that none of the body could be trusted.

gaum and Kolapoor. My force was increased by a battery of artillery, a squadron of dragoons, a wing of the 33rd (Duke of Wellington's own), and the remaining companies of the 2nd European wing. It would have been impolitic to have taken any more severe measures than I had done until strong enough to enforce them. The mutineer band in the Sawunt Waree jungles were being constantly hunted down through the active exertions of Colonel Auld, Political Superintendent, and his efficient local corps, chiefly commanded by Captain F. Schneider, brother to the Kolapoor Light Infantry Commandant, whose exertions below and on the Ghats rivalled those of his brother above.

I wish I could say as much for the Rutnagherry magistrate, but in all probability his brain was at the time disordered, and he afterwards committed suicide. Government partially remedied the mischief of his eccentricities by placing the police of his southern districts under me. It is due to him, however, to state that his thorough knowledge of native ways and languages enabled him to submit to Government important information, derived from intercepted correspondence in which treason hid itself under metaphor.

The Sawunt Waree insurgents of 1844 and 1845, who had sought refuge in Portuguese territory, and after having been for a while confined, had, when all was quiet, been set free by the Goa Government, with land for their provision, again, in February 1858, broke out in revolt, harried the country, and levied war in the name of the Peshwa (Nana Sahib). Their present leader, Baba Desae, was also practically chief of the former insurrection. It was satisfactory to me and to those who succeeded me at Sawunt Waree, the present Sir Henry Anderson and Colonel Auld, a district which, from our earliest connection with it, had been a hot-bed of insurrection, that now, when their old leader, with a hundred followers, traversed it with the hope of obtaining recruits, only one man joined him, and he not a native of the country. How many of the 27th mutineers and adventurers from all parts may, from time to time, have joined his band, I have no means of knowing;

but the pursuit was so hotly kept up that he had no time to gather strength.

Both the Bombay and Madras Governments, and also the Portuguese, employed troops against these insurgents, and so kept their atrocities within narrow bounds; but to detail their operations would render my narrative too long, and I must return to Kolapoor.

Not long after the affair in the town, wishing to know what Chimma Sahib would say on the subject, I requested him to pay me a visit, which he did. I told him that some had named him as the secret leader of the rebellion, but as I never acted on mere suspicion, he was safe as long as I had no proof of his guilt, for hearsay evidence was untrustworthy, and great men's names were often taken by others to shelter themselves; but I should be glad if he could give me any reasonable motive for the mutinous regiment having expected admission into the town, and for its having afterwards been surrendered to a small body of insurgents without opposition. He could offer none, contenting himself with protesting his innocence and ignorance of all the circumstances. I learnt that on his return to the Palace, the streets were crowded with women, cracking their finger-joints over their heads, and uttering cries of joy and congratulation at his coming back to them. I mention this for two reasons : one, as denoting his popularity ; the other as showing the belief of the people in his being the head of the rebellious movement. Hence their supposition that he would not have been allowed to return, and joy at his escape.

But just then I was not so well aware as the towns-folk, or rather, many among them, of his doings. By the end of March, however, the evidence of his complicity had become conclusive enough to convince me that it was dangerous to leave him any longer where he might work further mischief. By arrangement with Government, a frigate was sent down to the port of Waghotun, and when all was ready, he was requested to wait on the Political Superintendent, who had a communication to make to him on the part of Government. The gateways of the town were secured after his departure thence, with orders to let none pass out without permission ;

and the attendants and effects that he required being sent for, he was, during the night, removed under an escort of the 3rd Dragoon Guards, S. M. Horse, and Kolapoor Light Infantry, to the coast, with orders to make the first two marches in one. The commotion in the town was great as the news got wind, but none, however ardent, could sally to the rescue. Chimma Sahib was sent as a state prisoner to a safe corner of Sind, where he has lately died; and before I gave up military occupation of Kolapoor, I dismantled part of the fortifications, so as to render it accessible without running the risk that, at the exigency of the moment, I had incurred in forcing entrance.

I have mentioned the light gradually dawning on me from the confessions of military and civil prisoners, and that when the information from both agreed, there was sufficient ground for action. Thus it transpired that some time before the mutiny, Chimma Sahib had held secret interviews with the native officers of the 27th Regiment in the Royal Garden, conveniently situated between town and camp; also with a deputation from Gwalior, whence a body of sixty horsemen had come, nominally to congratulate the elder Raja on his marriage with the daughter of the Gaekwar, when those most trusted in the regiment were present, and the aspirations and designs of east and west interchanged. Chimma Sahib had also received emissaries from Nana Sahib, one of whom, who had travelled round by the south, coming last from Mysore, had informed him that he had secured the co-operation of forty different regiments. In reply Chimma Sahib bid him assure the Nana that he had gained over all the red-coated men in the S. M. country.[1] A sword[2] was also sent him

---

[1] In one of these interviews Chimma Sahib had remarked that he had not much hope of help from his own regiment (the Kolapoor Light Infantry), for 'Clarke Sahib had spoiled them with sugar and ghee.' On enquiring of Captain Schneider if he could explain this singular language, he replied that he had little doubt that the particular terms used, referred to the purchase by Captain Paget Clarke of a field of sugar-cane, for the use of the regiment, and generally to his liberal treatment of the men. I mention this, in justice to Captain Clarke, who raised the regiment, bringing into it many from his own corps, the 2nd Grenadiers, of which he had long been Adjutant ; and nearly half the present native officers were of that number.

[2] This sword was afterwards found in the Palace. It was silver handled, the blade of waving or serrated edge, covered with Sheeah inscriptions in gold. I regret to say that it was either lost or stolen by some of those intrusted to store away the arms.

from the Lucknow Durbar, and I had reason to suspect treasonable communication with several other quarters.

I was told that, on the morning I took the town, three emissaries from different S. M. States, who had been there, left precipitately. Treasonable intercourse also existed between the regiment and the country. The commander of the Jamkhundee troops was an active agent in the conspiracy, and proof was obtained of his carrying on seditious correspondence with our soldiery, on which he was tried and executed. A messenger from this man pointed out to me the house of a native officer of the 27th Regiment, to which he had brought a letter shortly before the mutiny.

But it is difficult to describe the wonderful secrecy with which the whole conspiracy was conducted, the forethought supplying screens, and the caution with which each group of conspirators worked apart, concealing the connecting links, and intrusting these with only just sufficient information for the purpose in view; and all this was equalled only by the fidelity with which they adhered to each other. As an instance, before the trial of Chimma Sahib's minister, a havildar of the local corps, an old friend of his, in whose quarter-guard he was confined, said to him, 'Why don't you make a clean breast of it? The Commissioner has let off many who have done so, and will perhaps pardon you too';' to which he replied, 'Were I to open my mouth I should kindle a flame to burn up the land. I choose rather to meet my fate in silence;' and he did.

In January, Colonel Maughan had been succeeded as Political Superintendent by Mr. A. D. Robertson, an excellent selection. The former was an honourable man of amiable temper and many good qualities, that at any other time would have enabled him to serve with credit; but it was his misfortune to have had only a slight knowledge of the language of the country, and no previous political training, and, still greater perhaps, to be surrounded by an establishment none of which gave any efficient assistance in the intelligence department of the State. I had information, indeed, long subsequently acquired, that the native most trusted by him, and who slept within call, in order to translate to him reports and papers that arrived during the night, had held secret interviews with Chimma Sahib, and one of Mr. Robertson's first tasks was to produce a more healthy state of things; but it was impossible to know whom to trust.

I have mentioned having employed half-a-dozen men to furnish a guard for my house at night. They were selected by our native minister in the town, under whose command were all the soldiery there. An additional motive for employing them was my hope, by means of friendly talk, of eliciting some information as to the state of feeling in the town.

The most intelligent of them I made their Naik (commander). This man had a brother in the post-office, and it afterwards came to my knowledge that both were in the conspiracy. Fortunately for me my man was seen in secret conference with Godajee Naik, the Raja's bodyguardsman, whose timely escape I have related, and was made prisoner in consequence. A party of armed men employed by the conspirators had lain in wait in a neighbouring garden for several consecutive nights, who were to have been admitted into my house under cover of darkness to murder me, as this man's help might give them opportunity; but his seizure appears to have put a stop to the plan. In like manner Captain Schneider narrowly escaped from a plot to murder him by a havildar of his own regiment, about sixty of which, it was ascertained, had been gained over.

Early in May Government struck the 27th Regiment off the Army List, retaining only for embodiment in another corps those who, from absence and other causes, might be supposed not implicated in the mutiny. These were marched to the coast to be sent away by sea, and of the rest some were imprisoned and others allowed to retire to their homes.

The elder Raja did not long survive the restoration of his kingdom. His successor, a young kinsman, trained in our schools, had been adopted on the death of his only child, Chimma Sahib's claim being of course forfeited. The premature demise of this

young man on his return journey to India is greatly
to be regretted, for he came to England solely to
improve his mind, and render himself more fit to
govern. It would be well if every Native ruler had
the same desire.

CHAPTER XII.

THE SOUTHERN MAHRATTA COUNTRY AND BELOW
THE GHATS.

EARLY in May Government placed the remaining States under me as Commissioner;
hitherto they had been under the Collector and
Magistrate of Belgaum as Political Agent, with an
Assistant, generally his senior subordinate, appointed specially for this duty. It was thought
advisable to secure unity of control in the present
state of affairs, and the Collector was directed to
make over charge to this officer, Mr. Charles
Manson, as Acting Political Agent under me,
Mr. H. B. Lockett being appointed his Assistant.

A brief description and *résumé* of events in the
Southern Mahratta Country will not here be out of
place. This part of India, as officially understood,
has an area of above 14,000 square miles, with a

population of some three millions. It is the territory between Satara country north and the Madras
frontier south, the Nizam's dominions east, and the
Ghats or Syadree chain of mountains west. Ethno-
logically it continues to the sea, from which to the
Ghats is called the Konkan. Below these the
people are all Mahrattas as far south as Goa.[1]
Above, the Canarese intermingle along the Madras
and Hyderabad frontiers up to the river Bheema,
spreading westward towards the Ghats.

In the time of the Peishwa, whose capital was
Poona, that city probably divided north from
south, the former extending till the people mingle
with those cf Guzerat. In Siwaji's time Satara
may have been the division, as it is at present, but
the term Southern Mahratta Country is of English
origin. It contains the two[2] collectorates of Belgaum and Dharwar, Kolapoor, already described,

---

[1] The Sawunt Waree people pride themselves on their pure Mahratta blood, that of the Bhonsle's. Their Raja, according to our
usual habit of metamorphosising words, is described in our old
treaties with this State as "The Bouncello!"

[2] Kaludgee, a subdivision of Belgaum, has since, I believe, been
raised to a separate collectorship.

and numerous small semi-independent States, not yet absorbed in the collectorates, each with an annual revenue of from 50,000*l.* downwards. The principal of these are Sanglee, Meeruj, Koorundwar, Jamkhundee, Nurgoond,[1] Moodhol, Savanoor, &c. Many of the people are warlike. All the descendants of Siwaji's Gudkurrees consider themselves born soldiers, and the Bedurs, Ramoosies, and Mangs, look on fighting as their profession, but the last two, deemed very low caste, only go in for it when there is a prospect of plunder.

Mr. Seton Karr was at this time collector and magistrate at Belgaum, and Mr. Ogilvy of Dharwar, while General Lester commanded the Southern Division of the Army, which had its head-quarters at Belgaum. It had been drained of its European troops for the Persian war, and, unfortunately, the three most recently-raised native regiments, viz., the 27th, 28th, and 29th, formed a portion of it, quartered respectively at Kolapoor, Dharwar, and Belgaum—unfortunately, because a new regiment

---

[1] Nurgoond was annexed to the Dharwar collectorate after the events about to be narrated.

is much more open to the temptation of disloyalty than older ones, with their military traditions and experience of the fostering care and power of our Government.

General Lester, an old artillery officer of sound judgment, had only recently assumed command. An account of the critical state of affairs at Belgaum, and of the measures he adopted to meet them, drawn up by him in October 1857, is well worthy of publication. I will not refer to it here further than to say that they had been in much greater anticipation of danger there, than at Kolapoor; at both stations the officers of the native regiments were confident in the fidelity of their men, and suspected no evil. The wise precautions of General Lester in all probability prevented an explosion at Belgaum. His only Europeans were a battery of artillery, and the depôt of Her Majesty's 64th, composed of about thirty men fit for duty, left with upwards of four hundred women and children. At Kolapoor, as before observed, they had neither artillery nor European soldiers. On the 10th of August the

European reinforcements, despatched from Bombay, reached him by way of Goa, arriving, as their brethren did at Kolapoor, in tatters, shoeless, and nearly kitless, from the severity of the monsoon, but eager for work. Strengthened by this reinforcement, he seized a few of the conspirators, civil and military, against whom there was sufficient evidence for trial. One of these was a moonshee, a favourite among the officers whom he taught. It appeared that he was a disciple of the head of the Wahabee sect in Western India, residing at Poona, who was a prime instigator of rebellion. Letters from the moonshee to the regiment at Kolapoor and other quarters, full of treasonable matter, had been intercepted, and furnished evidence against him. They showed the very wide extent of the conspiracy, and the readiness for a general rising when assured that other quarters would also move.

The discovery of this plot was mainly due to the zeal and energy of the Foujdar (native head of police) of Belgaum, a Christian convert, named Mootoo Koomar, who subsequently received the

grant of a village from Government, in acknow-
ledgment of his services. The moonshee was
found guilty, and executed, and with him an
emissary from one of the chiefs employed in cor-
rupting the Sepoys. Five men of the 29th were
soon afterwards convicted of mutiny, one executed,
and four, including the havildar major, transported
for life. In this case the same thing occurred as
at Kolapoor; although at the time the native
officers whose information led to their seizure,
were praised for fidelity, and the well-founded
distrust[1] felt by the local authorities being thus
removed, this regiment left Belgaum soon after

[1] To give the reasons for this distrust would make my narrative
too long, but as one instance I quote from General Lester's
memorandum. 'About the 13th of June (1857), a Sepoy's letter
was sent me from Bombay, intercepted there on its way to the
Bengal mutineers. It was written by a Sepoy of the 29th Regiment
at this station (Belgaum), and purported to be from several Sepoys to
their brethren of the 74th Bengal Native Infantry. They presented
their salaams, their protestations, their blessings, their Ram Ram, and
their Seeta Ram to all according to their respective positions.
"We are your children, do with us as it may seem best to you; in
your salvation is our safety. We are all of one mind; on your
intimation we shall come running. You are our father and mother.
We have written a small letter, but from it comprehend much.
You are the servants of Ruggoonath and we your slaves. Write to
us an answer as soon as you receive this." '

with flying colours for Aden, yet subsequent information established the fact that the accused had been thrown overboard as a tub to the whale by deeper conspirators than themselves.

It is not my intention to give a full history of events that occurred in the S. M. country previous to my assuming control, but, rather, to limit my relation to what came under my own cognisance ; a brief *résumé* is nevertheless necessary to connect the earlier with the later period of the rebellion in this part. When the Belgaum authorities felt themselves strong enough to change their defensive attitude for one of more active character, Mr. Seton Karr began the work of disarming the country, in the course of which, towards the end of November, the village of Hulgully, inhabited chiefly by Bedurs, offering resistance to a small force under Lieutenant-Colonel George Malcolm,[1] was stormed and many slain, a catastrophe that might perhaps have been spared had

---

[1] Now K. C. B. and Major-General, the same officer who headed the celebrated charge of the Sind Horse on the Affghan cavalry at the Battle of Guzerat.

Colonel Malcolm himself been in advance instead of his fiery Lieutenant,[1] whose *fortiter in re* was always more conspicuous than the *suaviter in modo*, but the conflict once begun had to be supported.

The affair showed the inflammable state of the people, and the danger that might accrue from the Forts, when a comparatively defenceless village could thus venture to oppose a Government force, however small. The example made in this instance had no doubt a beneficial effect in preventing further open resistance to the demand for arms, though secretion is believed to have been widely practised and the chiefs sent in their artillery very slowly, whilst the Shorapoor Raja, also a Bedur, began to collect men and prepare to fight. Troops were sent against him by the Resident of Hyderabad and from Belgaum early in February 1858; of the former Captain Newbury of the Madras Cavalry fell in a skirmish outside the town, which soon after surrendered to Colonel Malcolm's force. The Raja was made prisoner, tried, and sentenced

---

[1] Lieut. Kerr, who had won the Victoria Cross at Kolapoor.

to transportation for life. On his way to the coast he managed to obtain the revolver of the officer commanding his guard and shot himself. The confession that he made before his death was a valuable state-paper, throwing light on the general conspiracy. .

I have already referred to the outbreak of the old Sawunt rebels below the Ghats. They seized a strong position above with a view to connect themselves with the insurgents in the upper country. I have before alluded to this when speaking of the communication between their leader and one of the chiefs discovered by Captain F. Schneider. A force was sent against them under Colonel (now General) McLean from Belgaum and Dharwar, in the end of February, which drove them from their stronghold in time to allow the European troops to return in April to head-quarters, leaving the work to be carried on by native detachments stationed along the Goa frontier, and by the Sawunt Waree Local Corps and Police Contingent. All three deserve the highest praise for exertions and for trials endured, which none but those acquainted with the tremendous rainfall on these mountains during the monsoon can appreciate. It may seem invidious to single out any particular act where all did so well, yet I cannot refrain from mentioning the gallant defence of the Tulliwara Blockhouse, by a havildar and twelve men of the police. It may serve as a sample of the efficient work done by this body throughout the Presidency during the rebellion, but my narrative is restricted to the country under my surveillance.

The first efforts of the Sawunt insurgents were directed against the line of Customhouses on the several passes leading from British to Portuguese territory, some of which were destroyed and the occupants slain. Mr. Bettington, the able and energetic Commissioner of Police, had some time previously erected Blockhouses planned with military skill, to enable the defenders to beat off any desultory attack. That at Tulliwara, though not as perfect as he desired, resisted every attempt of the insurgents, who burnt down the Customhouse near, seized the families of the defenders, and even succeeded in setting fire to the Blockhouse. But still they were beaten back. Then the wives and children were brought in front by the rebels, who swore they would murder them unless the place was surrendered. The only reply won by the threat was that the British Government would avenge their deaths. The message of a holy man, sent with a flag of truce to induce the brave fellows to yield, was equally rejected, and the insurgents, finding every effort useless, left the place in the morning, carrying off their killed and wounded, and to their credit leaving uninjured the women and children.

Unhappily a delay took place in Mr. Manson's receiving charge of his office, so that he could not join me to report the past and present state of affairs, and to arrange further procedure, until the 16th of May. Some of the artillery and many arms yet remained to be delivered up, but he appeared to consider danger nearly over, and was anxious to visit the Northern States, as he had already before his promotion done those of the South and Midland, to judge for himself and to try personal influence with the chiefs.

The Putwurdhun family, which, in its several branches, held the principal States of the country, Sanglee, Meeruj, and Koorundwar, all within forty miles of Kolapoor, were allied by marriage with Nana Sahib, that is, with the Peishwa's family. Mr. Manson's influence was considerable from his frank and kindly disposition, and would have been still greater but for his previous connection with the Inam Commission,[1] which was looked upon with distrust and alarm throughout the country. It would lead me into too thorny a subject were I to enter into the amount of disaffection caused throughout India by the assumed right of our Government to disallow succession by adoption, a claim which the labours of the Inam Commission envenomed; suffice it to say, that of the many causes of the great outburst of 1857 and 1858 no single one was so weighty as this policy, happily now, I trust, for ever discarded.

Mr. Manson was in the prime of life, intelligent,

[1] A tribunal for enquiry into titles, with no appeal against its decisions allowed to any of the Courts of the land, but only to the Government by whom it was constituted, and to increase whose revenues it was working; a special Act being passed for this purpose.

energetic, and decided. He parted from me on
May 26, and four hours after I received from
General Lester a telegram that insurrection had
begun near Dharwar, and that the Nurgoond chief
was believed to be supporting it, as he had recalled
some of his guns on their way to be given up. I
immediately sent a horseman with this news to
Mr. Manson, informing him also that I had telegraphed to the General to send a competent force
with all possible despatch to Nurgoond if the
report proved correct ; and I recommended immediate return to Kolapoor to consult with me on his
way to join this force, to be with which was now
his proper position. My messenger reached him
at Koorundwar, and from thence brought me reply
that by cutting across country he could get so soon
to Nurgoond as perhaps to nip the evil in the bud
and prevent further mischief ; but that if too late to
effect this, he felt confident in being able to save
· the Nurgoondkur's half-brother, the chief of Ramdroog, from joining. From the moment of my
letter reaching him he had posted horses along the
road to proceed to the threatened quarter, and

before any answer of mine could again arrive at Koorundwar he would have been entirely out of reach.

On he went with great rapidity, leaving his infantry escort and establishment behind, and only taking with him a dozen troopers of the S. M. Horse, given him at Kolapoor. His hope was, that a letter he had despatched to Colonel Malcolm, commanding at Kaludgee, requesting junction at Ramdroog with a large body of his own regiment, the S. M. Horse, would have been received in time to effect this purpose; but on the alarm reaching that station, Colonel Malcolm with his usual promptitude had taken the field with 250 horse to attack the insurgents, who had plundered the treasury of one of the district stations of Dharwar; and Mr. Manson therefore reached Ramdroog with no other protection than his nearly worn-out troopers. From this place he sent me a few hurried lines, the last probably he ever wrote. 'I have come too late,' he said,—I quote from memory,—'the Nurgoondkur has thrown down the gauntlet and committed himself past hope of recovery, but I think I have saved the Ramdroog-kur, who has shown me his brother's letters urging co-operation. He conjures me not to go to Nurgoond, as in this case he will not answer for my life, so I go on to join Malcolm, who has gone southward after the rebels. My friend Poorun Sing, with a couple of horsemen, alone joined me here from Kaludgee. You should lose no time in putting an European garrison into Meeruj or Sanglee.'

That night, May 29, he pressed forward and halted at the little village of Soorebun, all parties probably exhausted from this rapid marching. No circumstantial account of what followed has ever transpired, further than that about midnight, whilst all were asleep, the Nurgoond chief sallied out with seven or eight hundred followers, horse and foot; and approaching close to the spot where his unsuspecting victims were lying, poured in a volley which killed the sentry, and rushed in to finish the work with the sword. Mr. Manson, roused from sleep in his palhee, fired his revolver at his assailants, wounding one, but was immediately overpowered, his head cut off and his body thrown into the still burning fire that had been kindled by his little party. Having killed all he could lay hands on, the chief returned with his bloody trophy to Nurgoond, where the head was suspended over a gateway. Some half-dozen stragglers effected their escape in the dark, but Poorun Sing, one of the best and most faithful officers of the S. M. Horse, fell with the young Englishman.

The insurgents against whom Colonel Malcolm had taken the field, proceeded rapidly southward, and took possession of the fort and town of Copaldroog, where they were speedily attacked by a Madras force under Major Hughes from Bellary, and the place stormed, when the leader and most of his adherents fell, a brilliant little feat of arms. Meanwhile, Colonel Malcolm turned back, and being reinforced by artillery and infantry from Dharwar, attacked the Nurgoond chief on June 1, defeated his force outside the walls with great slaughter, then and there carried the town by assault, and on the following day took possession of the citadel, a very strong one, but which on forcing open the gates was found deserted, the

Q

chief having escaped during the night. His track
was followed up with extraordinary energy, per-
severance, and skill by Mr. Souter, Superintendent
of Police,[1] with a few of his horsemen, and the Nurgoondkur, who adopted various devices for throwing
his pursuers off the scent, was, after a hot pursuit,
discovered, with six of his principal followers, in
a jungle, disguised as pilgrims on their way to the
shrine of Punderpoor. This was on June 2, so
rapidly was the outbreak quelled. He was soon
afterwards tried, condemned, and executed, and
his unhappy widows, unable to bear up under the
deep disgrace, drowned themselves. Speedily
and terribly was Mr. Manson's murder thus
avenged.[2]

The Nurgoondkur, Bhaskur Rao, or, as he was
more commonly called, Baba Sahib, was the most
intelligent of the Southern Mahratta chiefs. He had
collected an extensive library, reputed to contain
between three and four thousand Sanscrit volumes,

[1] Now Deputy Commissioner of Police, Bombay, and C. S. I.
[2] See a native poem on ‘The War with Baba Sahib,’ given in
the Appendix.

which was unfortunately destroyed in the sack of his town. It would be unfair to him not to state that he conceived himself grievously wronged by our Government, and it was this that probably drove him into the general movement of the time, before others more prudent, who held back till they should see the winning side. We had refused to sanction his adopting a son, and his State therefore, one of the oldest possessions in the S. M. Country, and not, like many, held on tenure of service, would, he knew, be absorbed by the British Government on his death, and his widows be left to depend on its bounty. As before observed, Mr. Manson as Inam Commissioner had incurred much ill-will, and it was he who had extracted from the Nurgoondkur the promise to surrender his guns, naturally looked on as a degradation. He was therefore identified with the policy of our Government in its harsher features, and became an acceptable sacrifice to the native discontent; but his relatives and friends have the consolation of knowing that he lost his life in the endeavour to save that of others.

A rumour of Mr. Manson's death reached me a few hours before I received his letter from Ramdroog, and I immediately took measures for controlling the northern States. Meeruj was the best fortified town in the country, European skill having been evidently employed on it, and siege guns appeared necessary for its reduction. I however deputed Mr. Lockett, on June 1, with my terms, demanding the surrender of all munitions of war and the admission of an English garrison. With Mr. Lockett I sent Lieut. Rollo Gillespie (now Major 106th Foot), a highly intelligent and daring young officer, a grandson of his celebrated namesake. He was to go nominally on a shooting excursion, but had private instructions to take unobserved a careful survey of the fort, and to pick out a good spot to escalade. As a stimulus to his exertions and prudence, I promised to give him command of the forlorn hope, intending to take the place by *coup de main*, should my terms be refused.

My plan was by a forced night march to reach the river that flowed near the town; there, by boats collected higher up, that were to drop down with the current to the spot selected, to cross at early dawn, and to take the fort by a sudden rush. All things in camp were prepared, and misleading directions to attract attention to other quarters given out. Happily Bala Sahib, the principal chief, after much hesitation and with great reluctance, yielded to the terms prescribed. But being a high-caste Brahmin, and most devoted to his creed, he expressed such horror of the desecration that would ensue from the drinking and beef-eating propensities of our soldiery, that Mr. Lockett, who conducted the negotiation with much skill, promised to represent this, and if possible have some arrangement made to avoid any needless shock to his religious feelings, meanwhile insisting on his at once giving earnest of his fidelity by sending in his arms and munitions of war. Eleven tons of gunpowder were taken from his magazines and exploded before Messrs. Lockett and Gillespie left the place, and many hundred bags of saltpetre and sulphur, war rockets, some freshly made up, and arms and munitions, sufficient for many thousand oldiers, were surrendered.

Bapoo Sahib Shapoorkur was at this time regent of the neighbouring State of Sanglee, during the minority of the chief. This Sirdar had lost seven villages through some flaw in the title found by the Inam Commission, but he was sagacious enough to see that he would gain more by joining, or at any rate appearing to join us than by opposition, wherefore, besides helping our commissariat with the loan of elephants, and in other ways, he now came forward to the rescue of the Meerujkur by offering to receive an European regiment at Sanglee, only a few miles distant. I consented to the arrangement on condition that at Meeruj a broad causeway should be made across the ditch to an entrance by a new gateway, and that part of the fortifications dismantled ; all which was in due time effected.

When visiting later all these places, I saw reason for congratulation that we had not been driven to use force, for Meeruj was a fortress of singular strength. The monsoon having set in, there would have been such delay in bringing up siege guns that I felt justified in the course I had contemplated ; but I took care before leaving that it should no longer be in a condition to render a regular siege necessary. I am happy to say that Bapoo Sahib was rewarded for his services to us by the restoration of his villages.

Mr. Lockett having been so short a time in office, I requested Colonel Malcolm to unite political with his military control until Government could make arrangements ; and Lord Elphinstone allowed me to call up Captain Frederick Schneider, who was well acquainted with the affairs of the country, to succeed Mr. Manson as a temporary measure. The southern States and trials were enough to occupy his full attention. In the north, Tasgam had recently been annexed by our Government, which had refused to acknowledge the adopted son, and it was natural to suppose that the disappointed widow would sympathise in any intrigues against us. But I could trace nothing beyond many religious mendicants passing to and fro, each ready to give a pious reason for his peregrinations. To check their doings, however, Mr. Rose spared me half a regiment from Satara, where troubles had quieted down, to garrison the place.

On the 3rd of July the southern division of the army had the misfortune to lose its commander by the sudden death of General Lester. On the 21st of the same month I was in orders as Brigadier-General, and soon afterwards became so seriously ill as to be obliged to leave for Bombay, the Governor kindly ordering the Civil Surgeon, Doctor Broughton, to attend me on the road. Before my departure I had the happiness of being able to report to Government that so far as regarded the upper country tranquillity seemed entirely restored. Below the mountains, along the Goa frontier, the Sawunt rebels still kept a large number of Madras, Bombay, and Portuguese troops, regular and irregular, in the field. On reaching the coast I slowly recovered a modicum of strength, sufficient to authorise the suggestion to Government that I should proceed to Goa to endeavour to procure a more efficient co-operation of the whole, and especially of that of the Portuguese Government, whose hearty assistance was all important. I further hoped that my influence with the Sawunt people might lead to the surrender of the insurgents. A frigate of the Indian Navy being appointed to convey me, I left Bombay on the 2nd of November, and was very cordially received at Goa by His Excellency, the Visconde de Novas Torres, an old general officer covered with scars and medals from the Civil Wars in Portugal. By opening his ports and facilitating the march of our troops to Belgaum, he had greatly assisted us; and now he consented to place the whole of his Field Detachments under the command of the officer who might unite that of the Bombay and Madras troops.

Brigadier-General Fitzgerald, and Mr. Ballard, Civil Commissioner of North Canara, were deputed by the Madras Government to meet me, and with Captain F. Schneider, and the colonel commanding the Portuguese Field Force, were present at interviews with the Governor-General, where plans of the campaign were discussed. But the difficulties of the country for military operations were so great that my chief reliance was placed on parties through whose influence on the rebel leaders I hoped to induce them to surrender, promising, on one hand, safety to life alone, while, on the other, I held out to them the certainty of harassment from all quarters and death either by military force or civil trial. To give them time for reflection, we suspended operations till the 20th of the month, after which date they were informed that they would be hunted down without mercy. I had the Governor-General's promise that when they gave themselves up he would deport them to the distant Portuguese possessions in Timor. I knew they would not trust themselves to our Government, but that of Goa had always behaved generously to them, and the only hope of success lay in acting through it.

Arrangements completed, we broke up the little Parliament. Brigadier-General Fitzgerald took command of the united forces, Captain Hewett commanding under him those of Bombay. The latter had been nominated to act as Assistant to Sawunt Waree and Belgaum agents, to secure united action of civil and military troops. Each officer took up his position, and I wended my way to Sawunt Waree.[1]

The rebel band had from desertion and repeated defeats dwindled down to eighty persons. These at midnight of the last day of grace surrendered to the Portuguese Commander. The Government of Bombay subsequently placed a war-steamer at the disposal of the Goa Governor-General, in which all whom it was considered wise to expatriate were shipped off for Timor, and the peace of the country for many years thus secured. Considering the important services rendered by this nobleman to our Government, I have been grieved to find that, notwithstanding Lord Elphinstone's acknow-ledgment thereof, and recommendation that some mark of honour should be conferred on him, they appear to have passed unrecognised.

The only published notice of these events I ever

---

[1] Sir Patrick Grant, then Commander-in-Chief of the Madras Army, came into the roadstead just as we were on the wing, the object being to give weight to our negotiations ; but finding all effected he passed on to Bombay without landing, the Governor-General politely going out to the frigate instead of inviting him on shore, as this might have prevented the insurgents surrendering from fear of being made over to us.

saw was in a local Indian paper purporting to give, under the heading of *Central India,* a telegram from 'The Political Commissioner,' whoever that gentleman might be, that, 'the rebel chiefs had surrendered;' yet several thousand soldiers were set free from a harassing campaign, the population along a line of 150 miles released from murder and pillage, and men who nearly from their childhood had kept the country in hot water deprived of further power of mischief.

All danger of further outbreak above or below the Ghats now being over, I resigned military command.[1]

I have now mentioned the principal events that occurred in the countries under my military or political control. It is somewhat remarkable that they should be so little known beyond the limits of the Bombay Presidency. Still more that they should have been denied by men whose position might have given them the knowledge from official

[1] As the Chief Political Authority, I reported to Government that the Field Establishments might be safely dispensed with. Three months afterwards I received an application from the Divisional Sub-Assistant Commissary-General, to whom the subject had worked its way down through the circumlocution offices, asking my opinion whether the thing could be safely carried out !

sources, but it is not the object of my present narrative to account for this.

On the 1st of November, 1858, the day before my departure for Goa, Her Majesty's proclamation to the chiefs and people of India came forth to supplement acts of severity by mercy. It was received with feelings never before evinced on any public occasion. I had the gratification of being present when it was read from the steps of the Town Hall in Bombay to the countless thousands who thronged to hear it, and during a forty years' sojourn in the East never witnessed such enthusiasm amongst a people by nature so undemonstrative.[1] In Western India Lord Elphinstone's government, and subsequently that of Sir George Clerk, carried out the spirit of the proclamation ; rebellion was pardoned ; despairing chiefs permitted to adopt sons ; and

[1] It must, however, be borne in mind that the Proclamation was chiefly appreciated by the upper and educated classes, by whom the lower, though apathetic, may be easily led or misled, and that with most the *omne ignotum pro magnifico* assisted in the feeling displayed. The power of the Crown was only known in the Presidency towns by its courts set up to control the local authorities. The Company's Government was always a mystery to the Natives, who have a keen appreciation of royalty, and under the gracious promises of the Queen it became a convenient scapegoat for past administrative evils.

Kolapoor and Sawunt Waree, with wise precautions and stipulations, restored to their reigning families. In the same spirit I have forborne to rip up old wounds now happily healed, and in this respect, as well as in some minor details of a painful nature, my history is purposely incomplete.

It will be sufficient if it help to convince the British people that there were more causes for the conflagration of 1857–58 than they wot of, and that a continuation of the policy of respecting native rights, rescued from doubt by Sir Stafford Northcote's administration, affords the surest prospect of future exemption from similar outbursts of pent-up hatred and discontent. As Bapoo Sahib Shapoorkur remarked to me on seeing the arrival from time to time of fresh European troops, 'What do you want these soldiers for now? Only act on the Queen's Proclamation and you may send them all back again as soon as you please.'

If our rulers are wise they will give its due value to such an expression of native opinion, and in their desire for progress cannot do better than act on the motto

FESTINA LENTE.

APPENDIX.

(*See page* 226.)

———◦◆◦———

Mr. Kies, a German missionary in the Southern Mahratta Country, gave Colonel, now Major-General, Sir George Malcolm the following translation of a Canarese epic, written shortly after the events related in my last chapter; it may interest as showing them from a native point of view. The poem must needs have suffered greatly from the attempt to put a literal translation into English verse, but the author has clearly intended to keep as near the truth as was consistent with his lights. The notes are not initialed by the translator.

THE WAR WITH BABA SAHIB
(THE CHIEF OF NURGOOND)
AND
THE CAPTURE OF THAT TOWN BY THE ENGLISH.
A.D. 1858.

I

The brave English, the great kings, took Nurgoond on earth;
The wicked chieftains were taken prisoners from their hearth;
The bad rebels were broken and fled in the midst of their
    mirth.
Have the English their equals?   To their power must stoop
    even Lady Earth !

II

Strife rose in the North ; searching swords, daggers, and
    diverse arms
Throughout the empire in towns, villages, and farms,
Besieging houses and creating alarms,
They came to Dharwar, with a great force collecting arms.

III

Many valiant lords with one mind there came,
To overflowing with anger was filled their frame ;
Gnashing their teeth they said, ' At which place must we aim?
' We have misgivings about that Fort, Nurgoond is its name.'

IV

The brave Chief of Police mounted his horse and joined his
    angry men.
They found out and brought arms from the rebel's den.
People who concealed swords, and yet denied it were beaten
    then
And pulled by the arm; to describe this I want a more
    powerful pen.

V

They came as victors, alighted at Nurgoond, gazed at the
    fortified hill,
And sat down thoughtfully to announce their will.
Baskaraja [1] was sent for and informed with skill
That his master must be disarmed. Hearing this, Baba fell
    down ill.

VI

'Why hesitate?' Give up arms, guns, powder and balls;
Do not conceal them in the ground nor in walls:
Give up all hope in this matter, and hear your master's call
To disarm your country! Do not sit idle in your hall!'

VII

At this command anger rose to the brain of the Chief; his
    eyes did glare,
Pouring forth sparks. On his body was bristling his hair

[1] A minister of the Chief, through whom he communicated with the
British Government.

R

With horror, but he curbed his passion and promised to disarm with care,

Saying to himself, ' If I am silent I shall better fare.'

VIII

He returned without stopping to his house with a wavering
mind,

Called his clever Minister, Raghopanta, and bade him with
calm mind

To consider well whether the promise given did bind

Him to collect and give up arms of every kind.

IX

According to his advice an answer was returned by Baba
the Lord.

' The arms are ours; we shall give neither gun nor sword.

Mark ! this is a clear answer to you. We have no other
word.

Be off in peace ! We have sent letters to gather our horde! '

X

Hearing this answer the Chief of Police [1] twisted his mousta-
chios and rose in a passion,

And said, 'Well done, Baba, thou art a traitor of a rare
fashion !

We shall soon come again to punish thy transgression;

Then I shall pour down thy throat molten lead without
compassion.

[1] The poet seems to have very misty ideas of the ruling
powers.—G. L. J.

XI

'Thou art like a straw; thou provokest the fire with open eyes.
Has the country been given to thee to devour it? In no
  wise!
Mark! thou hast eaten up thy measure of rice,[1]
Hero ! thou must not weary thyself by vainly boasting if
  thou art wise.'

XII

Instantly this message was sent to the great Collector,[2] on
  the excellent wire.
In a moment it reached the Court of the Queen, with the
  velocity of fire.
Here Mr. Manson was ordered to bring in the liar.
Obedient he set out ; he travelled on with haste, alas ! no
  more to retire.

XIII

He posted in every village on his road one horse ; went to
  Ramdroog with great speed;
Greeted Rao Sahib kindly and advised him to heed
The present time, to disarm and mount his steed
To go to Dharwar, where he would receive for his loyalty a
  becoming meed.

XIV

Rao Sahib gave to this advice a ready assent,
Mr. Manson left him smilingly and pitched his tent
Near Suriband. To go to Nurgoond was his intent.
Baba was informed of this by the spies he had sent.

[1] The time of thy death is near.
[2] See note 1 on p. 242.—G. L. J.

XV

Mr. Manson in his palanquin went to sleep,
Guarded by eighteen warriors who had to keep
Watch on his right and left side.   Of the secret wicked and
    deep
He had no foreboding.   Thinking of it we cannot but weep.

XVI

Baba came with one hundred men, foot and horse, like a
    shower;
They fell on the guards as tigers eager to devour.
They were killing to the right and left; there was no resist-
    ance to their power,
When Mr. Manson awoke—rose, and stood like a strong
    tower.

XVII

He saw the storm, and without hesitating fired off his gun;
But it was too late, there was none to help him, not one.
Baba seeing him called angrily to his men, ' My word must
    be done !
Cut him up quickly ! ' Thus the foul play was won.

XVIII

They returned to Nurgoond.   And going in procession they
    showed
The head of their foe.   Crowds of children and women
    cheering on followed.

Then it was fixed upon the gate.   The warriors assembled
    and bellowed,
'The foe has been caught!' So that with it the sides of the
    Hill echoed.

XIX

The next day Baba placed watchmen round the town,
Fortified the gate, prepared for war, and went down
To his warriors, gave them betel leaf,[1] and said, 'Frown
At my foes, saw them, make them sawdust, and uphold my
    crown.'

XX

Hearing this the warriors fell to the ground,
Beat the soil, and with a loud sound
Said, ' Father, take courage ! Do not doubt ; we feel bound
To defend you ! Our enemies will be soon cut up and
    ground !'

XXI

To which Baba, 'Tell me, where have they won a battle?
The coward English ! Are we afraid of their empty rattle?
They have taken countries with idle prattle,
But we shall weary them and offer their marrow to demons
    on the field of battle.'

XXII

Thus vainly boasting he was filled with gladness,
And prayed to his god to show kindness,

---

[1] Before beginning an important business betel leaf is distributed as
a kind of inauguration.

And deliver him mercifully from the sadness
Into which his enemies had plunged him with eagerness.

XXIII

Then he went to his Fort, his stores of ammunition ex-
    amined, and in secret places located.
His warriors received sugar and meal and were satisfied.
With the discharge of guns the air reverberated,
And the firm ground gave way and was agitated.

XXIV

He encouraged and explained all this to his wife :
' Be of good cheer and do not fear for your life !
Do not stab yourself with sorrow, that sharp knife !
God has brought this time, into his counsels you must not
    dive.'

XXV

The lady looking with sorrow on her husband's fate,
Said, ' What will be our lot after losing our place ?
We had better die !   'Tis a dangerous quarrel you dared to
    raise
With the English, this earth-conquering race.

XXVI

'But let be !   We shall not fear ; do not shrink in the fight ;
And wage war by the mercy of God with all might !
Hear, my husband, what I say, and prove a valiant knight
In vanquishing our enemies to our hearts' delight.'

XXVII

That foul deed perpetrated in the dark night-time
Was like a stain that cannot be effaced by white-washing
     lime.
It was a deed that could be pardoned in no time.
It was impossible that fortune should follow such a crime.

XXVIII

When our Masters in Dharwar heard of this murder it was
     as if a dart
Had been flung at them and fire poured into their heart.
They sent a message on the wire with art
And asked the Queen how the traitor ought to smart.

XXIX

This news flew with the swiftness of lightning to the far far
     West.
The Queen sat in Council, on the right and left to Her
     Ministers giving behest.
They heard it, beat the ground, bit their fingers, and smote
     on their breast,
Their eyes sparkling with rage, and roaring like thunder,
     ' Burn us ! We can have no rest,

XXX

' Mother Queen ! We must have revenge ! But God will
     extricate us ; do not speak words of grief.
Make haste ! Give order, and distribute to our warriors
     betel leaf,
That they go and lay waste the country of that Chief
Who is your subject, and holds that country only as a fief !'

XXXI

At this advice of Her Ministers, the Queen cast a gracious
    glance
On the august assembly, and ordered Her army with swords
    and lance
To go to the war, at which the soldiers began to dance
For joy, and asked, 'Where is Nurgoond? We shall cast
    that people into an awful trance.'

XXXII

The brave Colonel at their head was so full of ire
As to appear like a mountain ignited with fire,
From his eyes poured forth sparks of dire
Wrath, enough to consume such straw men as were in Babá's
    hire.

XXXIII

The first day they halted some miles distant from Nurgoond
    and alighted
To encamp. At dawn the officers rose, prepared for an at-
    tack, and were delighted
At the proposal of having their honour soon righted,
Mounted their horses and went on, at which Baba was sorely
    affrighted.

XXXIV

He prayed to Venkatramana, his god, to deliver,
Exhorted his men to attack, and not to shiver.
They sallied out gnashing their teeth like a rushing river,
At the sound of their drums the ground began to quiver.

XXXV

When the English saw them coming, they turned back their
    horse
Saying, ' Let them come forth ! ' And ordered their force
To retreat, and instructed them what course
They had to take, and put in readiness every resource.

XXXVI

Baba's men thought the English were flying
From fear. 'See how they run like horses shying !
They are broken ! Let us catch them ! ' the enemy was
    crying,
And followed to the brook, where the brave warriors in am-
    bush were lying.

XXXVII

Out rushed the soldiers, like a thunderstorm in an angry
    mood,
Their business to slay was well understood.
They surrounded and cut up this infernal brood
As a man with an axe is cutting a wood.

XXXVIII

As lions attack cattle and sheep, eager to eat,
The soldiers did not tire to cut, to stab, and to beat
These beggars who had no food, but were full of conceit;
They became now to the demons and fowls delicious meat.

XXXIX

Some were hiding behind trees, trembling ;

Others fled in disguise, dissembling,

Stumbled, fell, and with blades of grass in their mouths [1]
    were heard mumbling,

'O Englishmen, our Lords, do not kill us ! We are already
    like corpses tumbling.'

XL

Some threw away their arms with which they had fought ;

Others with much grief of their helpless wives and children
    thought;

Some unable to bear the heavy blows of the enemy were
    caught ;

All their arrogance and pride had come to nought.

XLI

When Baba saw his force shattered and broken,

He was confounded, and is said to have thus spoken,—

'O Bheemrao, O Chief of Dumbul ! [2] You have broken

The words which with an oath you had spoken.

XLII

'Perhaps my dull warriors did not well direct their guns and
    balls.

Alas ! they have deceived me ! .They showed courage only
    as long as they were within my walls,

---

[1] As a sign of surrender.

[2] The Insurgent Leader who fell at Copaldroog.—G. L. J.

These wily hypocrites! They betrayed me; that galls
My soul! They themselves are lost; to me they were false.

XLIII

'O Krishna! Am I not to thee devoted?
Was not thy worship always by me promoted?
What is my sin? On thee I have doted,
That I should lose my life can the Gods have voted?'

XLIV

Then he turned his horse and rode quickly to the Fort,
To which he thought his men would resort.
'Open the gate!' he cried, 'O God, the time is short!'
But none answered from within. He sighed and fled, that
  was no sport.

XLV

His wife hearing that her husband had been routed and put
  to flight,
Rolled on the ground, sighing and weeping from anguish
  and fright.
'What shall we do?' She asked her mother-in-law, 'how
  might
We have made our troubles and burden light?'

XLVI

Her virtuous mother-in-law wept when she heard this word,
And said, 'Before going he ought to have cut our throats
  with his sword.

Thus to leave and deceive us does not with his fine words
    accord;
We must go likewise, after we have been deprived of our
    Lord.'

XLVII

Both went and wandered about in the nearest wood,
Took each other by the hand, and went on without tasting
    food.
After seeing their efforts to find their Lord fruitless, they
    thought it best
To seek in the depths of the near river an eternal rest.

XLVIII

In the mean time the English, impatient to wait,
Rushed in through the unguarded gate,
And advanced to the Palace, moving on with fierce gait,
Crying, 'Seize, beat, stab, cut, let the foe feel our hate!'

XLIX

At not finding Baba they gnashed their teeth and researched
    the whole place,
But nowhere could they discover and recognise his face.
'Where can he be?' they exclaimed and began to gaze
At the Fort.   Hither was now directed the chase.

L

But they did not find him, and full of disappointment and
    rage
They said, 'Go where thou mayest thou wilt soon go off the
    stage!

That thou wilt escape destruction thou needest not believe!'
At their shouts of victory the hidden fugitives trembled like
    a withering leaf.

LI

The following day the Chief of Police permitted the soldiers
    to plunder!
The inhabitants were frightened and fled—no wonder !
The earth from the weight of the warrior's wrath cleft
    asunder ;
They shouted and roared like rolling thunder.

LII

Ten and ten went together, and thus through the town they
    were dispersed.
To deliver their swords, daggers, spears, and matchlocks,
    men were coerced,
Poor men were driven from their homes, and greatly dis-
    tressed :
But this is the lot of a hostile town, to be by victors
    oppressed.

LIII

In the houses of the bankers they took jewels, silver and
    gold,
Brazen vessels, iron, ivory, all was taken and sold.
In the huts of the farmers they took milk, butter and curds,
All kinds of grain, like preying birds.

LIV

They took and tied up in bundles clothes that had in boxes
    been kept ;
The women when seeing their garments taken, bitterly wept.
Braids, quilted garments, blankets and mats,—away all was
    swept.
There were many who in that night on the bare ground
    slept.

LV

But listen !   There was not left even to infants their cradle.
Yea they were denuded of their very swaddle.
From the kitchen was taken the ladle;
Oxen, cows, buffaloes, asses, sheep, were seized, and horses
    without saddle.

LVI

The butchers had to deplore the loss of their knives.
'Where are our cooking pots ?' lamented their wives.
Many wished that the warriors had taken their lives,
And sent them to that world where no sinner thrives.

LVII

Then 'he shops where cloth was sold were sacked,
The shops of spices were emptied.   None lacked
Food that day.   The bags of sugar and dates were unpacked;
They put dates one into the mouth of another, tasted and
    smacked.

LVIII

What they could not eat and could not carry was spilled,
After they had got their pockets completely filled,
Thereupon an old prophecy about the temple of Venkalestra
    was fulfilled,
That its idol would be broken and on its holy floor cattle
    killed.

LIX

Meanwhile the English searched all places where Baba
    might hide,
A fugitive he wandered near Torgall—gone was his pride,
A fire of anguish burned within him.   No guide
Had he in whom he could safely confide.

LX

When the soldiers came, and with skill surrounded
The place where Baba was concealed, he was confounded.
He tried to run, but a shower of balls fell on him; the charge
    was sounded;
The officers advanced; he was taken, and with their accla-
    mations the air resounded.

LXI

The great chiefs of the Army were filled with delight,
Saying, 'Our enemy has been caught !'   Many a traitorous
    wight
Was found there and ordered to be bound tight.
To bring them to Belgaum the officers exerted all might.

LXII

The people hearing that Baba Sahib had been caught,
Began to lament, saying, ' Fortune is fickle, power is fraught
With danger, empire is uncertain, woe to him by whom it
    is sought !
A noble chief has after a short reign come to nought.'

LXIII

Most virtuous kings, like Chola,[1] by Lady Earth[2] were
    deserted.
How often has she from powerful and mighty princes
    averted
Her face ! God only knows what she has secretly concerted !
Alas ! Baba desired such an unsteady spouse and was dis-
    concerted !

LXIV

He was virtuous, a man of renown, to little children a
    warden.
He was of a quiet temper. When seeing the poor he did
    not harden
His heart. He protected the brothers of science, the
    learned.
On festivals a rich harvest of presents by Brahmins was
    earned.

[1] A race of kings who ruled the Eastern coast of India about 800 years ago. From their name that coast was called Coromandel, i.e. Circle of Chola.

[2] Lady Earth is a personification of universal empire. She is courted by princes.

LXV

What times of trouble have come over such a great king !
How shall we forget such an awful thing !
With it our ears will always ring ;
We feel pain as if we were touched by a sting.'

LXVI

Men and women looked pale, and desired to see
Their Chief.   Strong men were shedding a sea
Of tears, and rushed out of the town
With women's bowels and hearts as soft as down.

LXVII

Our Lords in Belgaum received soon an answer from the
    Queen with glee,
That the traitor should be hanged on a tree,
When they saw Baba brought before them, with anger their
    hearts were filled,
'He is unworthy to live !' they said. 'He must be killed !'

LXVIII

While hanging him the rope broke ;
He fell to the ground and addressing his judges thus spoke :
'You are my refuge ; spare my life; put the cloak
Of mercy over me ; humbly I will bear your yoke.'

LXIX

It was of no avail that he suppliantly prayed and knelt.
At his words the hearts of our Lords did not melt.
They smiled, great was the anguish *he* felt;
But he was a murderer with whom they justly dealt.

S

LXX

Then other prisoners were tried and found
Guilty of death. To the mouth of a cannon they were
    bound,
And in a moment you saw in the air the fiery flashes—
Away to the eight points of the compass flew their ashes.

LXXI

Some prisoners had by a natural death been released.
After thus all rebels had been punished and justice appeased,
The heat of passion in our rulers' hearts cooled down and
    decreased
Till all angry emotions wholly ceased.

LXXII

The Ryots had been with fear of death excited
To leave the town ; they were now invited
To return. ' Remain ! Fear not ; we have plighted
Our faith to rule you so mildly that you will be delighted.

LXXIII

.' It is Baba whom you have to thank
For this happy change. Your town will now take the first
    rank
Among the places of the District ; we shall repair tank
And roads, and make you free and frank.'

LXXIV

Then our valiant masters united to give praise
To the LORD of the Universe for His goodness and grace,

That He had extricated them out of a maze
Of troubles, and guided them with the light of His face.

LXXV

'We fall down at Thy feet and worship Thee, O LORD;
Thou hast given victory to our sword.
We are Thy children, obedient to Thy Word.
Save us and protect us for ever, O LORD.'

LXXVI

The next day the grand army marched away
With smiling faces in battle array.
The drums were beaten, the pipers did play;
Arriving at the gate of the Queen's city they made a stay.

LXXVII

There met them the Mistress of the Earth who directs all
　　powers,
And headed the martial procession. The soldiers looked
　　firm as towers,
The grand Army marched through a triumphal Arch as
　　through bowers
Into the Capital that was decorated with garlands of flowers.

LXXVIII

As long as Sun and Moon are shining in the sky
No enemy will stand these heroes' battle-cry.
As wind and storm do chase the crazy butterfly,
So will an English host make all their enemies fly.

LXXIX

Thus the wicked rebels broke;
Riches vanished just like smoke.
Of this turbulent haughty race
Is not seen a single trace.

LXXX

Could the earth bear such great pride
Without gaping open wide?
Down they went with hearts right sore
Whence do men return no more.

LXXXI

Now has gone the powder smell;
On the ground lie ball and shell,
Tired of flying through the air.
People dwell contented there.

The Author clearly writes as one disapproving the outbreak, yet feeling sympathy for his countrymen; and this is what might naturally be expected from a Christian convert, or one *en rapport* with the Missionary. The general feeling of the population in the interior may be gathered from the following anecdote, told me by a gentleman high in the Civil Service, one well calculated, from the confidence he inspires, to ascertain the real sentiments of the native community, often very different from what they profess whenever they imagine a *couleur de rose* view agreeable to the enquirer.

'You ask me,' said a native to this gentleman, 'what the people really feel regarding the change of rule from the "Kumpany Bahadoor" to that of the Queen. As I know you wish me to speak the truth, whatever it may be, I will tell you by relating a story.

'Once upon a time a Dhobee (washerman) was washing his clothes in a lake, leaving his donkey as usual to browse by the side, when a thief came and took the animal away. By great exertion the Dhobee at last regained the creature, and having done so thus expostulated with it :—" Why, O ass, did you go away so quietly with that thief? If you had resisted, or only brayed to alarm me, I could have got to you in time to prevent it."

' "Master," replied the ass, "why should you expect me to care about it? As to food, I get what I can find. You load me as much as you think I can carry.

I should not be worse off in any change of masters, and I might perhaps be better."'

· This satire seems inconsistent with the enthusiasm mentioned in p. 237, but it has reference to the masses of the interior, who must never be judged of by the populations of the Presidency towns ; and the story was told after the first flush of the change had passed away and things were found to jog on pretty much as before.

FINIS.

LONDON: PRINTED BY
SPOTTISWOODE AND CO., NEW-STREET SQUARE
AND PARLIAMENT STREET

8vo., Illustrated, price ONE SHILLING;

Cloth gilt, Two Shillings and Sixpence.

PLEASURE:

A HOLIDAY BOOK OF PROSE AND VERSE

WRITTEN BY

Miss A. B. Edwards.	*The Hon. Mrs. Norton.*
Miss A. C. Hayward.	*Tom Hood.*
Author of 'Too Bright to Last.'	*Thomas Archer.*
Holme Lee.	*Godfrey Turner.*
Algernon C. Swinburne.	*Hain Friswell.*
Rev. Charles Kingsley.	*Countess von Bothmer.*

HENRY S. KING & CO., 65 CORNHILL.

Books of Indian Interest

PUBLISHED BY

HENRY S. KING & CO.

I

EASTERN EXPERIENCES. By L.
BOWRING, C.S.I.   Illustrated with Maps and Diagrams.
One vol. handsome, demy 8vo. 16s.

II

The EUROPEAN in INDIA ; with a
Medical Guide for Anglo-Indians.   By E. C. P. HULL and
R. S. MAIR, M.D., F.R.C.S.E.   One vol. post 8vo. 6s.

III

RUPEE and STERLING EXCHANGE
TABLES.   For the Conversion of Indian into English Currency and *vice versa*.   By DONALD FRASER.   Royal 8vo.
10s. 6d.

IV

A MEMOIR of the INDIAN SURVEYS.
By CLEMENT R. MARKHAM.   Printed by Order of H.M.'s
Secretary of State for India.   Imperial 8vo. 10s. 6d.

V

A CATALOGUE of MAPS of the BRI-
TISH POSSESSIONS in INDIA and OTHER PARTS
of ASIA.   Published by Order of H.M.'s Secretary of State
for India in Council.   Royal 8vo. sewed 1s.

☞ Messrs. HENRY S. KING & CO. *are the authorised Agents
by the Government for the sale of the whole of the Maps enumerated in
this Catalogue.*

LONDON, *October*, 1871.

A

ℭATALOGUE OF 𝔅OOKS,

PUBLISHED BY

HENRY S. KING & CO.,

65, CORNHILL.

A NEW CHRISTMAS BOOK.

Price One Shilling, 8vo, Ornamental Coloured Wrapper, from a design specially prepared, Illustrated.

PLEASURE:

A HOLIDAY BOOK

OF

PROSE AND VERSE.

WRITTEN BY

MISS A. B. EDWARDS.	THE HON. MRS. NORTON.
MISS A. C. HAYWARD.	TOM HOOD.
THE AUTHOR OF "TOO BRIGHT TO LAST."	THOMAS ARCHER.
	GODFREY TURNER.
HOLME LEE.	HAIN FRISWELL.
ALGERNON C. SWINBURNE.	THE COUNTESS VON BOTHMER.
REV. CHAS. KINGSLEY.	

WILL BE READY EARLY IN NOVEMBER.

65, CORNHILL,
October, 1871.

LIST OF BOOKS

PUBLISHED BY

HENRY S. KING & CO.

~~~~~~~~~~~~~~~

I.

EASTERN EXPERIENCES.

By L BOWRING, C.S.I., Lord Canning's Private Secretary and for many years the principal Commissioner of Mysore and Coorg. In one vol., handsome demy 8vo., illustrated with Maps and Diagrams. 16s.

II.

WESTERN INDIA BEFORE AND DURING THE MUTINIES. Pictures drawn from Life. By Major-General Sir GEORGE LE GRAND JACOB, K.C.S.I., C.B., Late Special Political Commissioner, Southern Mahratta Country, &c., &c., in one vol., crown 8vo, 7s. 6d.

III.

THE EUROPEAN IN INDIA.

A Hand-book of practical information for those proceeding to, or residing in, the East Indies, relating to Outfits, Routes, Time for Departure, Indian Climate, &c. By EDMUND C. P. HULL. To which is added—A MEDICAL GUIDE FOR ANGLO-INDIANS. Being a compendium of Advice to Europeans in India, relating to the Preservation and Regulation of Health. By R. S. MAIR, M.D., F.R.C.S.E., late Deputy Coroner of Madras. In one vol., post 8vo, 6s.

IV.

THE SUBSTANTIVE SENIORITY ARMY LIST,

of Majors and Captains in the British Service, in their order for promotion. By Captain F. B. P. WHITE, 1st W. I. Regiment. No. 1. 8vo, sewed, 2s. 6d.

V.

JOURNALS KEPT IN FRANCE AND ITALY,

from 1848 to 1852. With a Sketch of the Revolution of 1848. By the late NASSAU WILLIAM SENIOR. Edited by his daughter, M. C. M. SIMPSON. In two vols., post 8vo, 24s.

" The year which follows the fall of the French Empire and the final consolidation of the Italian kingdom is a most appropriate time for the publication of these 'Journals.' . . . The present volume gives us conversations with some of the most prominent men in the political history of France and Italy . . . as well as with others whose names are not so familiar or are hidden under initials. Mr. Senior had the art of inspiring all men with frankness, and of persuading them to put themselves unreservedly in his hands without fear of private circulation."—*Athenæum.*

" The book has a genuine historical value. . . . A suggesting commentary on the present state of affairs in France."—*Saturday Review.*

" No better, more honest, and more readable view of the state of political society during the existence of the second Republic could well be looked for."—*Examiner.*

" Will be read with interest by all Englishmen, and might be studied with advantage by all Frenchmen."—*Notes and Queries.*

" Of the value of these volumes as an additional chapter in the history of France at the period when the Republic passed into the Empire, it is impossible to speak too highly."—*Public Opinion.*

" It is impossible to imagine two volumes more instructive to read, or more replete with matter for reflection, information, and comparison."—*Civil Service Gazette.*

" To the student of this period the glimpse into the private opinions of the men whom Mr. Senior meets, will be both entertaining and instructive."—*Morning Post.*

" The Journals . . . . are interesting, and they appear at a peculiarly opportune time."—*Pall Mall Gazette.*

" Mr. Nassau Senior's journals, of which various portions have been at different times given to the public, possess very great value and interest, and we gladly welcome this further instalment of them."—*John Bull.*

VI.

ROUND THE WORLD IN 1870.

An Illustrated volume of Travels. By A. D. CARLISLE. Demy 8vo, 16s.

VII.

THE NILE WITHOUT A DRAGOMAN.

(Second Edition.) By FREDERIC EDEN. In one vol., crown 8vo, cloth, 7s. 6d.

" Should any of our readers care to imitate Mr. Eden's example, and wish to see things with their own eyes, and shift for themselves, next winter in Upper Egypt, they will find this book a very agreeable guide."— *Times.*

" Gives, within moderate compass, a suggestive description of the charms, curiosities, dangers, and discomforts of the Nile voyage."— *Saturday Review.*

" The subject . . . is treated from an original point of view, and we can safely recommend the little volume to public favour."— *Examiner.*

" We have in these pages the most minute description of life as it appeared on the banks of the Nile ; all that could be seen or was worth seeing in nature or in art is here pleasantly and graphically set down. . . . It is a book to read during an autumn holiday."—*Spectator.*

" Written in bright and pleasant style, and full of practical common sense."—*Notes and Queries.*

" Very pleasantly written. . . . An agreeable *compagnon de voyage.*"—*London Society.*

" This bright and clever little book."—*British Quarterly.*

" Useful for a traveller . . . extremely readable for a person who stays at home."—*Fortnightly Review.*

" Stored with useful information. . . . A very entertaining account of a very interesting trip."—*Illustrated London News.*

" Mr. Eden is a first-rate narrator. . . . His descriptive powers are of a very high order."—*Literary Churchman.*

VIII.

DISCIPLINE AND DRILL.

Four Lectures delivered to the London Scottish Rifle Volunteers. By Captain S. FLOOD PAGE, Adjutant of the Regiment, late 105th Light Infantry, and Adjutant of the Edinburgh Rifle Brigade. Fcap. 8vo, cloth gilt, 2s. 6d.

" One of the best-known and coolest-headed of the Metropolitan regiments, whose adjutant, moreover, has lately published an admirable collection of lectures addressed by him to the men of his corps."—*Times.*

" Capt. Page has something to say . . . . and in every case it is said moderately, tersely, and well."—*Daily Telegraph.*

" A very useful little book on a very important subject, and one which deserves the attention of Volunteers generally. The author is well known as a smart intelligent officer, to whose exertions the London Scottish is greatly indebted for its recognised efficiency."—*Notes and Queries.*

" The matter . . . is eminently practical and the style intelligible and unostentatious."—*Volunteer News,* Glasgow.

IX.

ASPROMONTE, AND OTHER POEMS.

Second Edition, cloth, 4s. 6d.

"The volume is anonymous; but there is no reason for the author to be ashamed of it. The 'Poems of Italy' are evidently inspired by genuine enthusiasm in the cause espoused; and one of them, 'The Execution of Felice Orsini,' has much poetic merit, the event celebrated being told with dramatic force."—*Athenæum*.

"The verse is fluent and free."—*Spectator*.

"We mention the book for its uncommon lyrical power and deep poetic feeling."—*Literary Churchman*.

"The poems are nearly all worthy of preservation."—*Nonconformist*.

X.

THE INN OF STRANGE MEETINGS, AND OTHER POEMS. By MORTIMER COLLINS. Crown 8vo, 5s.

XI.

SONGS OF TWO WORLDS.

By a New Writer. Fcap. 8vo.

XII.

A NEW VOLUME OF POEMS.

By PATRICK SCOTT, author of "Footpaths between two Worlds."

XIII.

THE SECRET OF LONG LIFE.

Dedicated by special permission to LORD ST. LEONARDS. Large crown 8vo.

XIV.

A New CHRISTMAS BOOK, Entitled 'PLEASURE,'

A Holiday Book of Prose and Verse, will shortly appear.

. *See Announcement on Wrapper.*

(5)

XV.

RUPEE AND STERLING EXCHANGE TABLES,
For the conversion of English into Indian currency and *vice versâ.*
By DONALD FRASER.
Royal 8vo, 10s. 6d.

XVI.

A MEMOIR OF THE INDIAN SURVEYS.
By CLEMENT R. MARKHAM.
Printed by order of Her Majesty's Secretary of State for
India in Council.
Imperial 8vo, 10s. 6d.

XVII.

A CHINESE AND ENGLISH DICTIONARY.
By the Rev. W. LOBSCHEID.
Royal 4to, cloth, 48s.

XVIII.

**THE PUBLIC WORKS DEPARTMENT OF INDIA—
WHY SO COSTLY?**
By Captain C. S. THOMASON.
8vo, sewed, 1s.

XIX.

**ON INNOVATIONS IN BANKING PRACTICE BY
CERTAIN OF THE AUSTRALIAN BANKS.**
Observations suggested by a recent Controversy in the *Times.*
By C. M. SMITH.
8vo, sewed, 6d.

XX.

THE FOUR-FOLD BOND.
By ROBERT CARR.
12mo, 2s. 6d.

XXI.

A CATALOGUE OF MAPS OF THE BRITISH POSSESSIONS IN INDIA AND OTHER PARTS OF ASIA.

Published by Order of Her Majesty's Secretary of State for India in Council.

Royal 8vo, sewed, 1s.

☞ Messrs. HENRY S. KING & Co. are the authorised agents by the Government for the sale of the whole of the maps enumerated in this Catalogue.

XXII.

THE BENGAL QUARTERLY ARMY LIST.
Sewed, 15s.

XXIII.

THE BOMBAY QUARTERLY ARMY LIST.
Sewed, 9s.

XXIV.

THE MADRAS QUARTERLY ARMY LIST.
Sewed, 12s.

XXV.

ETON HOUSE FOOT-BALL COLOURS, 1870-71.
Coloured Plate, containing 26 figures, 2s. 6d.

XXVI.

BRITISH POLICY IN CHINA.
By a Shanghae Merchant.
8vo, sewed, 1s.

NEW NOVELS.

I.

HER TITLE OF HONOUR. (Second Edition.)

By HOLME LEE. Author of "Kathie Brande," "For Richer for Poorer," etc. One vol., crown 8vo.

"It is unnecessary to recommend tales of Holme Lee's, for they are well known and all more or less liked. But this book far exceeds even our favourites, *Sylvan Holt's Daughter*, *Kathie Brande*, and *Thorney Hall*, because with the interest of a pathetic story is united the value of a definite and high purpose; and because, also, it is a careful and beautiful piece of writing, and is full of studies of refined and charming character."—*Spectator*.

"The graceful writer and accomplished lady who takes the name of Holme Lee as her *nom de plume*, has never written a more fascinating story than the one under the above heading."—*Public Opinion*.

"*Her Title of Honour* deserves in many respects to be ranked among the best of Holme Lee's works. It is a simple and unambitious story of every-day home life among ordinary English people, just what Holme Lee knows how to write; and she has done it in her very best manner. The characters are all strongly marked, well developed, and sustained throughout."—*Examiner*.

II.

HALF A DOZEN DAUGHTERS.

By J. MASTERMAN. Author of "A Fatal Error." Two vols., crown 8vo.

III.

CRUEL AS THE GRAVE.

By the COUNTESS VON BOTHMER. Three vols., crown 8vo.

IV.

LINKED AT LAST.

By F. E. BUNNETT. Translator of Auerbach's "On the Heights," &c. One vol., crown 8vo.

V.

IS SHE A WIFE?

By SYDNEY MOSTYN. Three vols. Crown 8vo.

VI.

MANQUÉE.

By the author of "Too Bright to Last." Two vols.

WORKS BY THE REV. STOPFORD A. BROOKE, M.A.

I.

FREEDOM IN THE CHURCH OF ENGLAND. (Second Edition.) Six Sermons suggested by the Voysey Judgment. In One Volume. Crown 8vo, cloth, 3s. 6d.

"Every one should read them. No one can be insensible to the charm of his style, or the clear logical manner in which he treats his subject."—*Churchman's Monthly*.

"We have to thank Mr. Brooke for a very clear and courageous exposition of theological views, with which we are for the most part in full sympathy."—*Spectator*.

"This plea for freedom in the Established Church is in some ways well reasoned, in every way well written."—*Nonconformist*.

"Interesting and readable, and characterized by great clearness of thought, frankness of statement, and moderation of tone."—*Church Opinion*.

"All who care for the progress of liberal thought will read it with profit."—*Examiner*.

"A very fair statement of the views in respect to freedom of thought held by the liberal party in the Church of England."—*Blackwood's Magazine*.

II.

SERMONS PREACHED IN ST. JAMES'S CHAPEL, YORK STREET. Post 8vo, 6s. Fifth Edition.

"No one who reads these sermons will wonder that Mr. Brooke is a great power in London, that his chapel is thronged, and his followers large and enthusiastic. They are fiery, energetic, impetuous sermons, rich with the treasures of a cultivated imagination."—*Guardian*.

"Mr. Brooke's sermons are shrewd and clever, and always readable. He is better off than many preachers, for he has something to say, and says it."—*Churchman's Magazine*.

"A fine specimen of the best preaching of the episcopal pulpit."—*British Quarterly*.

III.

A NEW VOLUME OF SERMONS
Is in the Press, and will shortly appear.

HENRY S. KING & CO., 65, CORNHILL.

TO APPEAR EARLY IN NOVEMBER.

PLEASURE:

A HOLIDAY BOOK

OF

Prose and Verse.

PRICE ONE SHILLING.

OCTAVO, ILLUSTRATED.

IN ORNAMENTAL COLOURED WRAPPER OF ARTISTIC AND ORIGINAL DESIGN.

See Second Page of Cover for further particulars.

HENRY S. KING & CO., 65, CORNHILL.

CPSIA information can be obtained
at www.ICGtesting.com
Printed in the USA
LVHW102046171022
730905LV00004B/334